Mrs Gwrak

Mrs Gwrak

Sweet Poison is her Weapon

A HORROR STORY FOR CHILDREN BY

MORGAN TOMOS

To Bobin and Carwyn

I would like to thank, of course, my parents, to a greater extent than usual in these cases, for their help. Also, the book is dedicated to my children for whom it was written. I would like to thank Guy and Jan for their enormous help and in particular John Lund for his invaluable help with the illustrations.

Thanks also to Eifion Jenkins and Eirian Jones.

First impression: 2011
© Morgan Tomos & Y Lolfa Cyf., 2011

Cover design: Morgan Tomos

ISBN: 9781847713056

FSC

Published and printed in Wales
on paper from well managed forests
by Y Lolfa Cyf., Talybont, Ceredigion SY24 5HE
e-mail ylolfa@ylolfa.com
website www.ylolfa.com
tel 01970 832 304
fax 832 782

Beware the power of the witch

Those whom the witch wishes to destroy, she first makes mad. It is the madness of a sweet poison. So beware the witch, for her time is now and she has the twisted wisdom of her ancient evil.

from the grave...

Three tons it weighed and yet it wasn't sucked into the muddy waters of the marsh. Its flakes of yellow paint, all but peeled away with rust, were dirty with the years of splattered mud from years of heavy work in that bleak, desolate place.

The noise of the digger, as its engine revved, was harsh and ugly in the still and empty quiet of the morning. The plume of dirty fumes from the exhaust was, for a moment, a black stain against the pale blue mist clinging to the marsh. But then the mist swallowed it into nothing.

It was always colder on the marsh. The cold clung like a spider's web to your skin. It sank into your bones and could not be shivered away. Even your eyes grew cold on that vast wetland. The cold was there in the pale empty blue of the mist, the dead green of the reeds and the deep, dark grey of the acidic water.

Even sound was muffled almost to nothing by the still water and the dirty roar of the engine seemed distant against the silence as it trundled over the swampy surface of the marsh. The sludge of acidic decay was squashed under the relentless power of its tracks but the machine did not sink. Finally, it reached the centre of the marsh. Here, the cold emptiness of the silence made sense. Shrouded by the mist, the marsh faded to a pale forever, and there was no other world but this. Not even sky.

But there was a ditch, dug many years ago to control the water level. Now it was blocked with silt. A vast pool of stagnant acidic water had spread and there was no telling how deep it might be. Bits of little dead things hung in the water; decaying very slowly and making it dark. You could not see where danger might be, where the mud was thin, where a man would sink without hope, sucked down deep to drown in dark water or be choked by mud – and leave no mark behind. Only a fool or an expert would ever tread the marsh so deep in water. And Bill Harris was no fool.

For years he'd worked the marsh. He loved it and could read all its signs. He loved to travel the vastness of it in his digger. His cab with large windows, high up above the enormous tracks, made him a king of that epic landscape. He loved the calm surface, the stillness of the bright pale mist against the darkness of the water. He loved knowing that the calm betrayed nothing of that deep, dark danger. But he also loved to go down onto the surface of the marsh itself, knowing where it was safe to tread, watching out for the details of life. Strange life. Life twisted into strangeness by survival on the marsh. There were the reeds, mosses and ferns – wet and brownish green and the flowers leeched of all colour with small petals held tight in a bulb. They were no great feast for the myriad tiny insects that lived a sparse life on the marsh. Ugly insects, like dirty brown skeletons, almost transparent, as if they'd drunk their tiny bodies full of the dirty acid water and used it for blood. To Bill Harris, this was not a place of death, but of life. It sprouted everywhere if only you took the time to watch. He understood that life thrived here because of the harsh acrid decay beneath the surface. The brown of the water seeped into everything, even the plants, and killed all colour dead. But the magic of the place was in the tiny, fragile details. Bill Harris would step down from his metal cab and get up close to the real fabric of the marsh and see every little struggle for survival. But for all his years of experience he couldn't understand why the ditch was blocked. It wasn't a very deep ditch. It wasn't meant to drain the marsh but to stop it flooding in heavy rain. There couldn't be anything large enough to block it. And yet there it was. A vast pool of water caused by a blockage. He was going to have to sort it out.

With painstaking care he moved the digger until he had it in the exact position for the job. It was worth taking the time to get it right. He didn't want the sides of the ditch to collapse, pulling him and his machine down into the water. But he had to get near enough to dig it out with simple strokes of the digger's arm and let the water flow away. He had to be patient. Centuries of careless death were imprisoned in the sodden mud of the marsh. Centuries of haste cut short by a sucking, drowning death. Patience and respect would get him through the job.

Finally he felt happy with his position and lowered the long metal arm into the silt, the teeth of the bucket slicing easily through the mud. It wasn't going to be all that difficult, after all. Just a matter of clearing the channel and letting nature take its course. He pulled on the lever to bring the arm up, expecting no resistance, but the engine groaned and the lever shook with the strain. That was strange. The teeth of the bucket had caught on something. He pulled harder on the lever and the arm inched its way upwards but the entire cab shook with the strain. He let the lever back down and took a short breather. Then, slowly easing the lever back, he tried again. But the more he pulled the lever back, the greater the strain. The cab began to shake again. He could feel the entire digger straining but he kept on at it. The vibrations grew to such intensity, he finally had to slacken the control once more. The shaking stopped. Bill Harris was breathing hard by now but he was determined. He loved his digger and the years of proud service it had given him. He and his machine were going to defeat this thing, no matter what.

With small, steady thrusts he dug the bucket deeper to get a better grip, then yanked it back in a show of strength that was meant to cut through the obstacle. The digger shuddered again and he felt it sink to one side. He pulled at another lever and the caterpillar tracks pulled the digger back, splattering mud onto the windshield but sinking it deeper-still into the marsh. He held onto the other lever with all his might and with a splurge of sludge the obstacle came free. A sudden rush of built-up silt and water hit the digger. It lurched wildly as the power of the sudden flow carried it to the edge of the ditch. All about him the marsh was sinking. He should have been scared. But he was too amazed by the object held aloft by the teeth of the digger's bucket and he felt no fear from the rushing waters. It was ancient and must have lain dormant for centuries, preserved intact by the waters of the marsh.

Bill Harris eased the pressure on the lever and felt the balance restored to his digger. With trembling fingers he turned the key to switch the engine off. For a moment there was silence. Then he became aware of the noise of swirling water. His eyes still riveted to the object, he opened the cab door and stepped onto the muddy caterpillar tracks. His knees felt weak but he had an irresistible urge to touch this thing; to feel the history of it and experience something from a different world long gone and lost in the mists of time. He lowered himself onto the marsh without checking that the ground was safe. The soft sludge pulled at his boots and made him struggle but he didn't care. He had to reach that strange object and touch it with his bare hand. It was a coffin made of thick lead. A sarcophagus.

The lid was shut tight but the lettering was visible. He gathered water in his cupped hands and washed the mud away:

Beware!

From hell itself she whispered her curse against us.
Clothed in seeming goodness was her vile intent
and here now she lies, her charred remains forever
drowned. Beware her corpse, for it can never die where
human life can feed her madness.

What could it mean? He had no idea but he knew he'd found something unique and of immense value. Every museum in the world would want to have this and his name would live forever as the man who'd found it. He was going to be rich. He deserved that much at least after all his years of thankless work on the marsh.

He knew what he was supposed to do. He should leave it alone and report his find to an expert. That was the proper thing to do. But there was something irresistible about it, something fascinating that drew him towards it. He reached out and felt the edge of the lid with his fingers. It was smooth and rounded. There was craftsmanship in the making of it. On all four sides were carved symbols he couldn't understand. But one thing was clear to him; those carvings were warnings to leave this thing alone. They warned of a supernatural danger beyond human understanding. As the water ran down the casket, it revealed further writing in smaller letters. Harris could tell at a glance that they told a story. He cleared away the mud and read:

We are but humble farmers, or were, for we hope we are long dead when these words are read and our story told. Do not open this coffin, for it contains an evil beyond life.

For three years we had endured one bad harvest after another and we faced not just hunger but starvation. There seemed no reason for the crops to fail and the animals to wither away and die, diseased in the fields where they grazed on grass turned brown by drought and scorching sun. All about us a kind of lifeless pall hung over our village and made the very air heavy and difficult to breathe. The river had run dry, but when the rain came it washed away the soil in a torrent that drained our very lives into the poison of this marsh. Hunger gnawed at our bellies but the hunger of our children drove us mad as well. We prayed without hope for a miracle.

And then, as if from nowhere, she came to our village. She was a strange woman. Some of us felt uneasy in her presence but she promised our deliverance. She had remedies for our animals and powders to put in our soil and soon there was fattened livestock in our fields and the promise of a harvest beyond our wildest dreams. We were thankful for her charity and many felt she was great. We fell into her trap of hope, for we had to wait for our reward. To wait in hope and fear for the fruits of that harvest made us want and want beyond reason – and that made us vile. When our crops were almost ready and bulging with life the strange woman asked us, 'And where is my reward?'

At first we didn't understand her. There would be a harvest so great we would gladly give her a share of it. The greatest share. But that was not to her liking. 'Where is my reward?' she demanded again and some of us gathered the fattest animals and harvested some crops that seemed ready, to show her that we would share with her. But that would not do. The crops withered and turned to dust as soon as they were collected and the animals died a bloodless death at her feet. 'Where is my reward?' she demanded again and this time she looked towards the children. It was a look of death and we knew what she desired. 'I only want the eldest from every family,' she said and some of us, those whose eldest child was a girl, readily agreed – that was vile. But some of us did not agree. We said so, and that night she left our village. At that moment the heaviness returned and we all knew that the crops would fail. A group of us went to find her, to beg her to return even though it meant our children would die. But she had to be appeased or else it would be death for all. The shock of it, to those children who were eldest, was too great to bear. Some were thrust at her feet and some ran away to hide but we found them. Some of us refused to give up our eldest child. We clasped them to our bosoms but they were wrenched from us. We were told not to be so selfish as to deny the good of all for the sake of the few. We bowed our heads in shame.

But some of us knew that next year the eldest would be asked for again. And again the following year. There would be no hope of children. We were buying life with death and would end with nothing. A few years at most was all the life allowed from then on for any child and life, though lived, would be a curse. We, who saw the death behind her promise of life, were wise enough to keep silent. She despised us and felt no fear, and so we planned against her, trapped her and put her to the flame. We were hated for it by all those who had given themselves to her power but we kept certain death away from their children as well as our own. Do not open this coffin. It contains your death. You have been warned.

Harris rubbed his chin and rolled his tongue around his mouth. The warning wasn't for him. People of olden times had strange beliefs that meant nothing now. It was just superstitious nonsense. And, if he reported his fantastic find he would never get a proper look inside and see this supposed evil from a bygone age. Experts would take it away from him. They would get all scientific and self-important and they'd barely thank him for finding it in the first place. They hadn't been grateful to him before when he'd discovered other odd relics from the past; a bracelet or some coins or a leather purse from Roman times.

Experts! What did they know of the real work he did on the marsh? What did they know of the dangers he faced day in, day out and without reward except a pat on the back? Let any one of them come down here and see for themselves. Let them walk the marsh. See if they could handle the danger of a hell beneath their feet. A cold, wet, dark hell. A hell of total disappearance.

No. He was the real expert. He knew the marsh better than them for all their so-called scientific knowledge. This find was a treasure and it was his. He was going to be the first to look inside. He'd report it to the experts eventually but until then this thing belonged to him. And he was going to do as he pleased.

He set his feet apart and grabbed the lid with both hands. When he was sure he had a proper grip he pulled. It was heavy and jammed by centuries of slow decay in the waters of the marsh. He pulled again, harder this time and he felt it give a little. He pulled harder again and this time it really did start to open. He rested a while, catching his breath for a final effort. Then he gripped the lid tightly with both hands and heaved. There was a scraping noise and water began to seep out of the casket. He heaved again and the lid swung open.

He gasped at what he saw. It was almost a skeleton, half burned, although the waters of the marsh had been kind to it and preserved much of its skin and flesh – mummifying the corpse. But the skin, preserved as it was, clung wetly to the bones and to the skull in particular. It had shrivelled onto it and turned a deep and decayed brown. The lips had rotted away, revealing only a few stumps of teeth in a mouth that smiled its rotten putrefaction at him. The eyes were closed and shrivelled deep into the sockets, the lids crinkled into deep creases that travelled from the sockets and along the cheeks and temples. He started to laugh with amazement. He knew how rare this was. Rare? No such thing had ever been found before. He was going to be famous and yes – he was going to be rich. He fumbled for his mobile phone, unable to contain his excitement. He was desperate to tell someone about his incredible discovery. But before he could dial the number the corpse opened its eyes and stared at him. They were perfectly preserved and pierced him with their cold, grey stillness.

Neither he, nor his machine was ever seen again.

prepare

A frog leapt out of the food and landed with a plop of thick gravy on the table. Mr Williams stared at it, his knife and fork quivering in his grasp, his eyes bulging with shock. The frog stared back at him with its own bulging eyes. In all his years as headteacher he'd never seen such a thing. Or heard of anything like it. It was an outrage! Miss Lauren couldn't believe her eyes either. She looked at Mr Williams. His eyes were still bulging, his lips and jaw slack and his body rigid. She could see his temper rising on his face. The frog gave a happy croak and leapt again. Mr Williams blinked and went straight into action. He stood up, looked at Miss Lauren and shouted:

'MISS LAUREN! CATCH THAT FROG!'

That was a mistake. They were in the school canteen and the children were whispering to each other as usual instead of eating their food. The whispering had grown louder and louder until it almost sounded like talking because all the children had to whisper louder and louder to compete with the noise of all the other children whispering louder and louder. Usually, when the noise grew too loud, Mr Williams would shout out: 'You can't be eating very much because there's far too much talking!' Or: 'Quiet in the canteen! I can barely hear myself think!' What he really wanted to shout was:

'SHUT UP!'

Children weren't allowed to talk and eat because they made too much noise and the teachers couldn't hear each other talking while they ate. They would have to shout and eat and they would spit bits of food at one another. When that happened, Mr Williams would wipe the bits of food off his face and shout:

'THERE'S FAR TOO MUCH TALKING AND NOT ENOUGH EATING!'

The children would shut up and then he could carry on eating and talking with the teachers. That's what usually happened. But when Mr Williams ordered Miss Lauren to catch the frog, he used his big SHUT UP voice.

'MISS LAUREN!' he'd shouted. 'CATCH THAT FROG!'

All the children heard it and fell silent. Did he say 'Catch that frog'? Then Mr Williams turned to the other teachers and in his loudest SHUT UP voice said:

'THAT FROG LEAPT RIGHT OUT OF MY FOOD!'

The roar of laughter from the children hit Mr Williams with a force that almost threw him back onto his seat. He stormed round the table.

'THIS IS NOT A LAUGHING MATTER!' he shouted but that only made things worse.

'I AM YOUR HEADMASTER AND I DEMAND SILENCE!' he roared as he went from table to table, his face sweaty with rage. But he hadn't noticed the frog leaping behind to follow him about. Mr Williams marched up to a table of children and shouted and threatened and banged the table until they bit their lips to stop laughing and turned red in the face. But hop, hop, hop, the gravy-plopping frog followed him about and the laughter flared up again the moment he turned his back. Thump, thump, thump on the table. Roar, roar, glare, glare. Silence. Back turned, hop, hop, plop, plop. Roaring laughter! Gales of laughter, bigger and louder than before.

When he finally caught sight of the frog, he was ready to explode with rage. He turned to the table of teachers. None of them had helped him. Did he have to do everything himself? He pointed at Miss Lauren and shouted above the roar of laughter:

'MISS LAUREN! I THOUGHT I'D TOLD YOU TO CATCH THAT FROG!'

She was already on her feet and now she hurried towards the little creature. She cupped her hands and bent down to catch it with ease.

'Thank you,' said Mr Williams sarcastically. He turned to face the children, to finally put an end to their noise. But before he could exert his full authority, Miss Lauren showed the frog to the children at the nearest table. It was cute and its head was poking out between her fingers. It had big, shiny eyes and a drop of gravy on its head, like a little hat. The children at the table fell silent and craned their necks to get a better look. The other children also stopped talking and leaned forward. Very soon the sound of laughter died away and the children ooooh-ed and ahahahahah-ed as Miss Lauren showed everyone the frog. Then, she took it outside and released it. The canteen was now a warm, happy, calm place. The only sound was the gentle murmurings about just how gorgeous that little frog was. Everyone was so happy and delighted.

Mr Williams was furious. He was the headteacher! It was his job to restore calm. How dare Miss Lauren steal his job! But he couldn't give her a row for succeeding. Instead, he would have to thank her. He ground his teeth with baffled rage.

Mrs Jones the cook and the two dinner ladies popped their heads out of the hatch.

'What's wrong, Mr Williams? Did you say something about a frog?'

'Aha!' thought Mr Williams. He could give *them* a row! He marched into the kitchen.

'Frog, Mrs Jones?' he shouted. 'Frog? Yes I did say something about a frog – a frog that was in my food!'

Mrs Jones and the assistants reeled back in shock. None of them had put a frog in the food.

'Was it cooked?' asked Mrs Jones.

'Cooked? Of course it wasn't cooked! It leapt out of my food!'

'Honestly, Mr Williams. I don't know anything about it. We were making the pudding.'

'Is it a frog pudding, Mrs Jones?' asked Mr Williams sarcastically. Mrs Jones and the dinner ladies were

shocked. There was no such thing as a frog pudding.

'Let's take a look at it then!' thundered Mr Williams and he lifted a large, glinting carving knife. Mrs Jones rushed forward.

'Please, Mr Williams. Stop.'

'Stop? Are you preventing me from checking the pudding, Mrs Jones?'

'No, no, Mr Williams.' She put her hand gently on his arm. 'But please don't do it this way, in this accusing manner. We're very proud of the food we make.'

The headteacher relented. Perhaps Mrs Jones was right. He might have gone a little over the top. He lowered the knife.

'I'm very sorry, Mrs Jones. There was a frog in my food. It was very distressing. I'm not accusing you but I must examine the pudding.'

'Of course you must, Mr Williams. By all means, carry on.'

'I'm sure it will be in perfect order and delicious as usual.'

He cut through the block of sponge, releasing a cloud of hot, sweet steam. They breathed it in and sighed with satisfaction. Everything seemed fine until the worms curled out of it – a wriggling, writhing mass of shiny, steaming pink worms that slithered in slippery knots, coated with crumbs of sponge. All four of them staggered back at the disgusting sight.

'Are they poisonous?' asked Mrs Jones.

'Poisonous?' said Mr Williams. 'You should know!'

Mrs Jones was about to protest her innocence but just then the children started screaming. Maggots and spiders, cockroaches and all sorts of insects came crawling out of their food and a horrible stench invaded the canteen. In the kitchen, snails came sliding out of the saucepan of custard... followed by a black snake.

The Visitor

It wasn't the dust dancing in the sunlight or the patch of peeling paint on the ceiling of the classroom. Not today. Today it was the cars going by on the road outside. One by one or in rows they went by with a distant noise and a flash of colour. David wished he was in one of them, travelling far away from school and yet another lesson on a subject he knew nothing about.

The school was in a small town in the country, large enough to have a few shops but nothing special. Not like in the city, quite a few miles away. David knew from watching telly and what he saw on the internet that a city was exciting. Things happened there. Nothing happened here. And even if it did, who would care? Aliens could invade and nobody would take any notice. There was talk of a new factory and that was it. His dad was hoping to get work there. That would be nice. Nice. That just about summed it up. David was bored. He always felt bored in the afternoon when he was stuck in a lesson. He could see the school gates in the distance, so far away and closed against escape.

Then, out of nowhere, she was just standing there; a tall, thin woman with long white hair tied in a severe bun at the back. David instinctively drew back from the window. He could still see her – he couldn't take his eyes off her – but he didn't want her to see him. Her dress was dark. It flowed like a dense black cobweb down from her shoulders. She was somehow surrounded by darkness. It flowed out of her like a miasma with her at its centre. A still centre. As the cars whizzed by, swirling dust and dead leaves in their wake, even her dress stayed absolutely still. And the dark vapour slowly swirled about her like smoke on a still day.

The centre of her stillness were her eyes. Their stillness was deep and yet alive with a kind of fury; a strange, boiling, icy fire full of unremitting malice.

David felt sharp pain in the palms of his hands. He looked down and saw his hands were balled into tight fists. He felt the pain as his nails dug deeper into the skin. But such was the instinctive fear that he couldn't unclench them. Cold sweat swept over his forehead and he looked up again. The woman reached down to open the gate with a hand, whose long fingers ended in nails as sharp as razors and dirty with deep decay. She walked across the yard towards the school with a strong, steady step.

He didn't feel the gentle tap of the book on the top of his head. It was Miss Lauren. David had been caught again, daydreaming in class, staring out of the window instead of listening. But he couldn't take his eyes off the strange woman. Miss Lauren felt a surge of anger. She was always catching him out and the routine was always the same. Everybody else was working hard or paying attention and Miss Lauren would call out his name. He never responded

to that. His trance was always too great. Then she'd kick off her shoes and sneak right up to him. And all eyes would be riveted on this performance. She would tap the top of his head with a book or gently say his name right into his ear. And he would wake up. But this time, it was worse than anything he'd done before. He was completely ignoring her.

'Are you paying attention, David?' she asked right into his ear. But his gaze remained fixed on the woman.

'David!' she shouted and that broke the spell. He looked up at her, his eyes blinking in puzzlement.

'Huh?' he muttered as he realised at last where he was and that he'd been caught again. Then the roar of laughter hit him. The blinking eyes, the puzzlement and the dumb 'Huh?' were better than ever – absolutely perfect.

From the second Miss Lauren had noticed David staring out of the window the entire class had waited for this moment, looking forward to the stupid 'Huh?' Even his best friend Gareth was laughing at him along with all the rest of the class. But his laughter was friendly; not like Adrian's nasty, hacking laugh. He was always in trouble himself and he liked nothing better than to see someone else get told off. Of the whole class, Annette was the only one who wasn't laughing. She was far too sensible for that. She just shook her head in disappointment and rolled her eyes. Wouldn't he ever learn? But Jemma, her best friend and David's sworn enemy, was laughing at him; her eyes gleaming with nasty satisfaction. As for that big gang of boys, the lads, they were howling with laughter and David knew they'd be taunting him in the playground at break time. It wouldn't last long but it would be loud as usual. Then they'd find something better to do like break the rules or out-boast each other. But that smaller set of girls who were always so very, very good were looking down their noses at him and sneering. Naughtiness was going to be punished and they loved it. They were never ever, ever, ever, naughty.

'I've had enough of this daydreaming,' said Miss Lauren at last and the class fell silent. 'Go to see Mr Williams.'

David realised he'd gone too far. It was no wonder Miss Lauren had finally had enough. But how could he explain? Who would believe him? Who would ever believe he'd seen a witch walk through the gates of the school?

David stood in the corridor, trying not to be noticed. It was always embarrassing to stand in the corridor outside the headteacher's office. Teachers going past would stop and ask why he was there and what had he done. Repeating the reason over and over again was the worst of it. He looked down at his shoes, trying not to be noticed or even pretending that he wasn't there at all – that was the only way to handle it.

There were voices coming from inside the office but David couldn't hear what was being said. One of the voices belonged to Mr Williams but the other voice was female. He just hoped it wasn't that woman. He'd calmed down a bit since he'd first noticed her. She couldn't really be a witch but he was petrified at the thought of seeing her close up. The door opened and Mr Williams saw the woman out.

'Goodbye for now and I'll see you tomorrow,' he gushed as he held the door open. David had never seen Mr Williams hold a door open for anyone before, not even parents.

'And thank you so much, so very, very much.' David had never seen Mr Williams being so servile. He was usually very rude with everyone.

She stepped out of the office and David pushed himself hard against the wall. It was her! Close up, that uneasy feeling gelled into a paralysing fear that crawled across his skin. She *was* a witch! The blackness of her dress robbed the corridor of light as it cast a shadow beyond itself and into the very air around her. The material brushed against him as she walked past and David shrank back as if it was diseased. He pushed himself harder and harder against the wall.

'I'll see myself out,' said the woman. Her voice was not hostile or commanding. It was a voice that simply expected to be obeyed. She looked down at David as she went by; a casual glance at something beneath her notice. He tried to hide his primal fear and hoped she'd mistake his trembling for a more general shame, the shame of being sent to the headteacher. She looked away again and he breathed a sigh of relief. But then she turned her head back towards him and David averted his eyes. He'd seen a glint of something else in her eyes; something terrible – interest. 'Oh, please don't take an interest,' he panicked inwardly. 'Just go away as if I wasn't here. Please don't see how terrified I am. Just go.' But he felt her gaze upon him.

'Here is a perfect example of what I was saying,' she said to Mr Williams. David still felt her gaze on him.

'This boy is too thin. He has no health. Are you healthy, boy?' she demanded and David was forced to look up. The moment their eyes met there was a flicker of recognition. She knew! She knew he could see that she was a witch! Her steady gaze drilled into him and he felt a strange, floating sensation. He felt he was drowning. The witch was inside his head. Was she reading his mind? No! Please, no! She mustn't know he could see through her disguise! The floating feeling increased and David surrendered to it. The woman's eyes filled his vision. He could feel the depth of it; a bleak, empty depth, draining his thoughts as into a vacuum. As he was about to fall, the floating feeling suddenly stopped. The woman stood up straight and carried on down the corridor, leaving in her wake a cold, dark emptiness that seemed to suck the life out of all existence. Had she read his mind? Did she know everything about him? Was he safe?

Mr Williams looked down at David and snorted.

'So it's David Roberts again, is it? I guess you've been daydreaming again instead of paying attention.' But David wasn't paying any attention to him. He was still looking at the woman as she seemed to glide gracefully along the corridor.

In all his years as headteacher, Mr Williams had never seen anything like it. It was an outrage. Here he was, giving a boy his most fierce row in his best headteacher voice for not paying attention and the boy wasn't paying attention to him!

'David Roberts!' he shouted again but David hardly heard him at all.

The woman reached the door and smoothly left the school. With the click of the door David woke from his trance and noticed Mr Williams at last. His face was bright red and tinged with purple, the veins on his temples and neck bulging like thick rubber tubes.

'I've been shouting your name!' Mr Williams shouted, his voice squeaking with the strain as it always did whenever he totally lost his temper.

Oh, no. He'd done it again. Mr Williams had caught him out again. This was serious.

'Get into my office!' he roared. David went in as Mr Williams collected his breath from all that shouting, straightened his tie and pulled his jacket back into shape, ready to give the row of his life.

Inside the office the monitor from the CCTV

cameras was switched on. Mr Williams really liked his CCTV cameras. He'd probably been showing them off to the woman. Ever since they had been set up he'd been able to boast that breaking school rules was now impossible. Their cold, silent, remote eyes would always see you if you were naughty. This had impressed the boys – and straight away they'd set out to find where the cameras could see and where they couldn't. These areas of the playground, blind to the eye of authority, became highly prized and were dominated by the bigger boys. Those goody-goody girls who were forever competing against each other in an everlasting war of goody-goodness were also impressed. These cameras would catch bad behaviour and offer proof that they were right to complain (as they always did, all the time, to all the teachers, about anything and everything and even nothing if they felt in a really goody-good mood). But Mr Williams had soon disappointed them (although he didn't mean to).

'But if you're good,' Mr Williams had said as these very, very good girls preened themselves – they knew he was talking about them and they were really pleased – 'If you're good and well behaved then the cameras will ignore you completely.'

He'd meant it as a warning for all the children to behave well but the very, very good girls huffed with a livid rage. Being good wasn't about being ignored! Being good was about reporting badness and receiving praise from a teacher! How could a camera do that!? It couldn't! The very, very good girls snorted in disapproval. It just wasn't fair.

David watched the woman on the monitor screen walking across the playground. She stopped at the gates and turned to look back at the school. He was startled. On the monitor she looked just like a kindly old lady. That air of evil was totally gone and her smile was broad and generous. Was that her secret? Was that why Mr Williams couldn't sense her character as he could? The cameras showed her as an ordinary, generous old lady and perhaps that's how Mr Williams saw her too. But then why had he been so servile towards her? He'd cringed and fawned at her. He'd almost bowed down to her with a sweaty smile. Surely the woman David saw on the monitor screen could not have made him do that. But David knew that she had. He'd seen it with his own eyes. And the worst of it was that if he ever tried to explain – then no one would believe him. David understood all too clearly the secret grip this witch already had on the headteacher. He was scared of her. Some primeval instinct told him to be scared. But he also thought she was good. That was the power of her disguise.

That night, fear of the witch kept David awake. He told himself over and over that it was all in his imagination! But it was night-time now and the darkness put a grip of fear on his heart. Only the power of his mind stopped him from cowering in the corner, waiting for her silent footstep beside his bed.

In the end he did drop off but sleep brought with it a nightmare he could barely endure. He was outside the headteacher's office and the witch came to eat him as Mr Williams stood waiting impatiently. He could feel the pressure of her gums and stumpy teeth as he was swallowed into the darkness of her mouth. And then her shadow fell on Miss Lauren as she taught her class. David was at his seat as the witch stood between them and pointed down at him with a long, knobbly finger. She was that kindly old woman again but her smile was full, foul, open-mouthed and false. David wanted to shout, to warn them all against her but her smile mocked him, daring him to shout out his warning. It would be the worse for him if he did. He couldn't hear what Miss Lauren was saying and he knew he would be caught for not listening and sent to see Mr Williams again and the witch would eat him once more.

He felt himself say 'Huh?' and the laughter of the children echoed in his brain and that was the final straw for Miss Lauren, who turned on him in anger. The witch stood in the middle of the classroom, daring him to speak out. He mustn't say anything or they would think he was mad. That was her power and David bit his lip to stop himself from shouting a warning to them all. The witch laughed, a heckling laugh that sliced through him like a blade – daring him to speak out and show his madness to the class.

He woke with a silent scream of terror coursing through his blood. Dawn had arrived and shafts of sunlight broke into the dark bedroom through the slits in the curtains. David realised he was safe in bed, that it was only a nightmare. But the fear still clung to him. He forced himself to feel safe and at home. Slowly, he calmed down and began to see sense. His heart still pounded in his chest but he convinced himself to be reasonable and to realise he'd let his imagination get the better of him. After all, what had the woman done? She'd stood looking at the school, she'd gone to see Mr Williams and she'd looked down at a boy, a naughty boy who was waiting outside the headteacher's office. That was all. The rest of it was all in his head. Perhaps he really had gone too far this time. The daydreaming and strange ideas would have to stop. The camera had shown him exactly what she was – a kindly old woman. And David had thought she was some kind of monster. A witch. That would have to stop. After all, everyone knew there was no such thing as a witch.

strange food

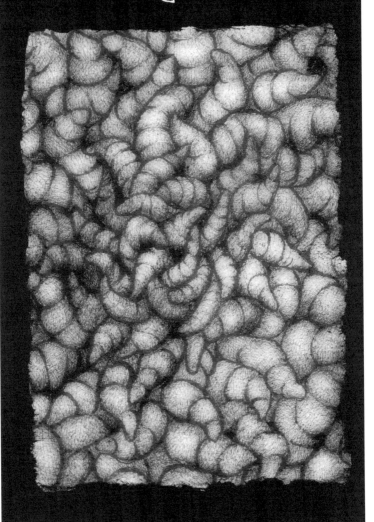

It was almost lunchtime and a new cook was starting that day instead of Mrs Jones. Everyone hoped she was a good cook who would make lots of the good foods they liked and less of the healthy foods they were forced to eat. When the bell rang for lunch, all the children walked smartly out of the door. As soon as they were out of sight they pushed and shoved for their seats in the canteen. As David was about to join the rush, Miss Lauren gently called him back.

'David? I'm really proud of the work you've done today. I was beginning to despair of you.'

Oh, no, thought David, she was going to talk nicely to him. And she might take a lot of time doing it. Didn't she know it was lunchtime? The time of day when you didn't have to do schoolwork. Didn't she know he needed to get in there to push and shove for his place? Couldn't he ever win? If he was bad, he was sent to Mr Williams. If he was good, he was kept away from his food!

'You want your lunch, don't you?' She smiled indulgently at him. 'I know it's the best part of the day and I don't want to keep you from it.'

Unbelievable! Totally unbelievable! Why did adults do this, and especially teachers? She knew he wanted to go. She'd said so, but she was keeping him there, asking him questions about wanting to go for his lunch! Unbelievable!

'I am looking forward to it, Miss Lauren,' said David, raring to go but trying to hide it.

'Well, off you go, then,' she replied, as if David had been the one dawdling and wasting time. As he crashed through the door she called out:

'And remember, I'm very proud of the work you've done today.'

When David reached the canteen a powerful golden smell of sickly sweetness struck him full force. The air seemed to be full of fine, savoury sugar and even the smell of it melted in the mouth like an actual taste. But David didn't like it at all. Underneath the savoury sweetness he sensed a stale smell of decay that clung to his nostrils and repelled him.

When he looked about the canteen he saw and heard the strangest thing. Everyone was open-mouthed with their tongues hanging out, their heads lolling from side to side like cattle. The usual sound of loud whispering had gone. Instead, all David could hear was 'Ungungung' as all the children licked the air, trying to get all the savoury-sweet flavour onto their tongues. Huge globs of saliva dribbled from every mouth and every eye had a dull, gormless look.

David made his way towards his best friend Gareth who was lolling his head from side to side like everyone else. Luckily there was an empty seat beside him but Gareth didn't even notice when David sat down. Adrian was on the same table – his thick tongue licking the air.

'Are you going to do that all the time?' David asked Gareth.

'Ungungung,' was the only reply he got. Then he noticed that David wasn't licking the air.

'Ungungung, ungungung?' he asked. David turned away in disgust, the sound of 'ungungung' throbbing in his ears.

The door of the canteen flapped open and David saw Miss Lauren walk in. At first she was surprised by the pleasant smell. Then she crinkled her nose. She hated the sickly smell just as much as he did! As he watched Miss Lauren's reaction he knew why the savoury sweetness was so powerful. The food itself must be rotten.

Miss Lauren saw the children lolling their heads from side to side, rolling their tongues and going 'ungungung'. She looked towards the table of teachers and saw them licking their lips and grinning stupidly. They wanted to loll their heads about and lick the air just like the children. But they were teachers; they had to look respectable. She strode towards them and started arguing with Mr Williams. But he just smiled and waved her away. She sat down, a furious look on her face. David knew that look only too well; he'd seen it often enough in class.

Mr Williams got to his feet and tapped the table with a fork. All the children turned their heads to look at him but the 'ungungung-ing' didn't stop.

'Right,' he shouted above the noise. 'We can all smell that delicious cooking.'

The sound of 'ungungung-ing' rose in a firm agreement.

'Today we have a new cook instead of Mrs Jones who… who… well, we all know what she did and we can put it out of our thoughts. Erase from our minds the frog and the worms, the snails, the cockroaches, maggots and snakes. There's no need to recall that disgusting event at all, however vividly it is seared into our minds forever. We can forget it. And forget it we shall, however much it may live in our memory forever more. Because today we have a new cook instead of the disgusting Mrs Jones and her filthy creepy crawlies. Her name is Mrs GwraK. And before we eat, I'd like to introduce her. Mrs GwraK!' he called to the kitchen, 'Could you come out here for a moment. I'd like the children to meet you on your first day.'

The side door of the kitchen opened and out stepped a tall, thin woman. The moment she entered the canteen the ungungung-ing stopped as if silenced by an axe. It was her! The new cook, who was preparing all the food for the whole school, was that strange woman! David peeped over to look at Miss Lauren. She was frowning, not just with her lips. Her whole face was frowning. Her brows were knitted and her eyes were narrow. David had never seen her anger that intense. It wasn't just him. He wasn't the only one to sense that nasty air of evil about the woman. Miss Lauren felt it too. David realised he'd been right all along. How else had all the noise disappeared? There was adoration, worship even, in the silence inspired by the woman. That proved he was right!

Mr Williams was equally taken aback by the sudden silence. He'd geared himself up to shout above the noise but the sudden ceasing of the 'ung-ing' had tripped him up. His mouth flapped open and shut as he couldn't find any words to say. He turned to Mrs GwraK for support but she was intent on the children.

'I'd like to welcome Mrs GwraK to our school,' stuttered the headteacher at last, aware that nobody was really listening to him. Then he turned to Mrs GwraK. 'Perhaps you can say a few words to the children.'

She stepped forward and smiled sweetly at their expectant faces, though her eyes were like glinting slits of cold contempt.

'Thank you very much, Mr Williams.' Her voice dripped with the same sickly sweetness as her food. But David could hear the real tone of rasping hate beneath her false kindness.

'I look forward to my task of cooking delicious meals for you. And I can see you're all eager to get at the food.' There was a sudden 'ung-ung' of agreement.

'Yes, yes! Thank you Mrs GwraK,' said Mr Williams, smiling at her cravenly.

'I'll let Mrs GwraK get on, shall I? I don't know about you but I can't wait to taste this food.'

Mrs GwraK gave a sly smile and was about to return to the kitchen when, out of the silence, a single child began to cry. David couldn't see his face but it was one of the younger boys.

'She's a witch,' he cried in a trembling voice. 'A witch, a witch, a witch!'

Miss Lauren was on her feet but Mr Williams had seen her.

'Stay where you are, Miss Lauren. I'll handle this.' He hadn't forgotten that episode with the frog and the thought of it still made him furious. David saw the look of anger, frustration and anxiety on Miss Lauren's face but she reluctantly sat down. The headteacher laid into the child.

'How dare you say such a thing you ungrateful, spoilt brat! It's an outrage!' he shouted into the boy's face. David could see the poor boy was trembling with fear but Mr Williams kept on, his anger rising and bursting out. 'You will apologise to this lady and then you will leave this canteen!'

In a smooth, almost gliding movement, Mrs GwraK was by the headteacher's side. She laid a hand on his shoulder.

'There's no need to be so harsh, Mr Williams. I forgive him and I won't deny him any of my delicious food. After all, I've prepared it especially for all these lovely children. And for you also, Mr Williams, the headteacher, and your staff.'

David saw the headteacher puff himself up.

'Feed one, feed all is my motto,' she beamed at him.

'That is most gracious of you, Mrs GwraK.'

'Not at all.' She bent down and cupped the child's face. He cringed away but her grip was firm. 'Is there something about me that makes you afraid?' she asked tenderly, though the cold threat of her eyes was plain for David to see. In fact, with her mouth smiling and the tone of her voice dripping with kindness, the icy threat was all in the eyes. It pierced into the child.

'Are you afraid of me?' The child shook his head rigidly and Mrs GwraK stood up straight.

'There now. Am I frightening?' The boy shook his head vigorously. Mrs GwraK gave a satisfied smile. She turned on her heel and glided back towards the kitchen. Mr Williams scuttled after her.

'Rest assured, Mrs GwraK,' he called out to her. 'If anyone else insults you, I will give you my full support, my fullest support.'

Mrs GwraK was already through the side door to the kitchen and closed it in his face. Mr Williams turned to the canteen-full of children and teachers. He chewed his lower lip in embarrassment and straightened his tie. He had to reclaim his authority somehow.

'I hope all of you here understand that our new cook will not be treated with disrespect and will receive my full support,' he thundered at the children. However, his words were lost as from the moment the side door was shut the 'ungungung-ing' had resumed with even greater force and no one was listening to him.

David tried to attract Miss Lauren's attention. She was aghast at what she'd just seen and was trying to catch the eye of the boy who'd called Mrs GwraK a witch. But he was too frightened to look towards the teachers' table – the last place he expected to get help. He turned round in desperation to the other children, trying to find somebody, anybody who'd seen what he'd seen: a witch in the school canteen. David avoided his pleading look. He couldn't help him, dared not help him. The child was exposed, known to the witch. What could David do but bite back his shame and wish, wish, wish that this was not happening? He was a coward and there was nothing he could do about that. Nothing.

The boy turned back to his table and tried to join in with the noise of 'ungungung-ing', trying to be normal like his friends. David was glad to see the back of him. He couldn't bare those pleading eyes. David had no power. None. But he felt the shame of doing nothing.

The 'ungungung-ing' increased as the queuing began and the food that smelt so delectable got nearer and nearer. Table by table, the children rushed to fill their plates and when they got it they howled like monkeys and couldn't wait to stuff great globs of it into their faces.

David prodded his serving suspiciously. It was

a fried pat of golden brown sludge swimming in a syrup of congealing fat. Close up it looked like a wriggling mass of brown maggots smelling of sugar and overpowering putrid rot. It was disgusting. He looked across at Miss Lauren who was sitting bolt upright with a look of disgust on her face. She only toyed with her food, pushing it about her plate. He looked around the canteen and saw that everyone else was stuffing themselves. Even the boy who'd said Mrs GwraK was a witch was slowly eating his portion. But David could tell he wasn't enjoying it. The only other person not eating the food was Annette. Sensible Annette. She and David had always been friends even though they were so different. Nobody had ever called David sensible and Annette was always amazed at the trouble he got himself into. She didn't look as disgusted with the food as Miss Lauren, but he could tell she didn't like it. He put his fork down.

'Don't you want yours?' asked Gareth. He'd almost finished his share.

'I don't like it.'

'What!' Gareth gaped at him and David saw the bits of food stuck between his teeth and on his tongue.

Adrian had wolfed his own food in an instant and was just licking his plate clean when he saw David hadn't eaten any. Without asking, his big paw reached out to grab it. But he was too far away. His hand slapped uselessly on the table. Gareth was quick. He slammed his arm down, blocking Adrian who glared at him. Gareth glared back and Adrian took his revenge. He grabbed the last of Gareth's food and stuffed it in his mouth. As he licked his hand, he smirked at Gareth who sprang to his feet in fury. Gareth was big, but Adrian liked to fight. He was always so angry and he always won.

David pulled Gareth back down to safety in case a teacher noticed. He darted a glance towards their table at the far end of the canteen – the teachers weren't about to notice anything. Apart from Miss Lauren, they were all intent on the food, especially Mr Williams. He'd stuffed most of his food in both cheeks. A huge stupid grin split his face from ear to ear as he chewed his way through it. His skin had turned pink with pleasure and for a moment he actually did look like a pig.

David scooped all his food onto Gareth's plate. Now Adrian glared at David.

'Give me some of that!' he threatened.

Before David could answer, Gareth said: 'No! It's mine now! You stole my food and I'm not giving you any!'

'You wait,' snarled Adrian, 'You wait!'

bad feeling

After lunch, David wanted to find Annette and talk to her about the food, and find that boy to give him some comfort. But he had a job to do. Adrian was prowling the playground, waiting for his chance to get Gareth. The food had made Gareth dozy and all he wanted to do was wander about in a trance. David kept him close to the school building where it was safe.

'David?' asked Miss Lauren from behind him. 'Have you seen Graham?'

'Graham?'

'You know. The boy who…' Miss Lauren hesitated. 'The boy who got a bit upset at lunch.'

David knew who she meant but he hadn't known the boy's name. He saw the worry in her eyes but she quickly looked away and the silence between them was laboured. They both knew – but they couldn't say – what they were thinking. Graham had said it. He had said it out loud. He was too young to know any better. He'd blurted out his fear, cried for help – and made the witch notice him and smother him in a false, threatening niceness.

'You're very lively compared to all the other children,' said Miss Lauren, trying to find something to say. But it was true. She'd never seen the school playground like this. All the children were so quiet and listless, as if they were in a boring lesson, not being given the chance to play. There wasn't any shouting or laughing or running around. The children weren't even speaking to one another – just hanging about, staring blankly into space. She felt it must have something to do with the food and since David was the only one behaving normally, she wanted some answers.

'Did you enjoy the food today?'

'Miss, I didn't even like the smell of it.' He was a little bit worried about admitting it because you never knew how a grown-up would react. They could be so awkward. David was surprised by her reaction. She was pleased.

'I could see you didn't like the food either,' he added.

'Yes. And I thought I was the only one – apart from Graham.'

'Annette didn't like it either, Miss.'

Miss Lauren looked even more pleased. David wasn't surprised. Annette was bound to be a favourite with any teacher. She always did her work quietly and gave the right answer to every question every time. Her mind never drifted off to some faraway place when she should be paying attention. She was the perfect pupil.

'She didn't like the food. I could tell. But she did eat it,' said David.

'Did you give the food back?'

'No, Miss. I gave it away.'

Miss Lauren thought about this for a moment.

'You make sure you eat something good when you get home.' Then she added, almost to herself, 'I've never seen food like that before.'

David knew she was breaking the rules by complaining about school food to a pupil.

'Miss Lauren?' he stammered, afraid of the words he was going to say next. 'I thought the new cook looked a bit like a witch.'

'You shouldn't say that.' It was a reprimand, but her voice wasn't harsh.

'I only said she looked like a witch,' insisted David.

'You shouldn't even think a thing like that,' she replied trying more and more to be the teacher. At last she added: 'Tomorrow, I'm bringing a packed lunch. You might like to do the same. Now, I'm going to find Graham. I think he needs some help.' She walked off towards the playing fields.

By the time David turned back to look for Gareth, he had gone. David ran to the field as fast as he could. There was no sign of a fight. No crowd of boys yelling or anything like that. Then he saw him. Without any commotion or shouting, Adrian was pounding his friend with his fists. Gareth had his arms up to defend himself but it was no use. Adrian was in his usual fierce temper and Gareth was in a worse stupor than usual.

As he ran towards them, David shouted for Adrian to stop, but he ignored him. David grabbed him by the shoulder, but he just carried on smashing his fists into Gareth. David stood back helplessly as his friend, bloated and full after a double portion of food, puffed out cries of pain as Adrian hammered him. David had no choice. He stepped forward and punched Adrian on his back with all his might. Adrian spun round, his eyes blazing with anger. David hit him again and he fell back but David was too stunned by what he'd already done to follow through. Adrian recovered and attacked full-force. He had a way of shooting one punch after another, his arms like pistons. David grabbed his arms and wrestled him, stopping him from punching hard. That was his only chance. They grappled each other but David knew it was only a matter of time before Adrian would break free and really hit him. Adrian had already grabbed his collar with his left hand and was frantically trying to release his right arm from David's grip. He jerked his arm backwards and forwards and bit by bit, David's hold gave way. Then David felt a hand grab his shirt, pulling him back. The other hand pushed against Adrian's chest. It was Miss Lauren, and she was angry.

'What do you two think you're doing?' she demanded.

'It was the food,' said David.

'Don't use that as an excuse. I was kind to you and this is how you pay me back!'

'Adrian was beating up Gareth! I had to do something!'

She turned on Adrian. 'Were you fighting Gareth?'

'No. David hit me from behind.'

Miss Lauren felt her heart sink. It was always the same when boys got into a fight. He did this. No, he did that and it's not true. Getting at the truth was almost impossible.

'Gareth? Did Adrian attack you?'

Gareth stood there looking stupid.

'I don't know,' he answered in a happy sing-song voice.

Miss Lauren turned her glare back at David.

'Miss, I gave Gareth my food,' he protested. 'He's had two portions!'

She knew what he meant. Gareth had very dull eyes, even worse than the other children. She was more than ready to believe David but then Jemma stepped forward. She had a nasty look on her face and he knew that meant trouble. Jemma was best friends with Annette but Annette was also friends with David. Jemma hated David.

'Miss Lauren,' she said. 'I saw David hit Adrian from behind. Then he tried to run away.'

'Did you see Adrian fighting Gareth?'

'No, Miss. I didn't. David hit Adrian from behind and then he tried to run away.'

'Oh? When David ran away, what did Adrian do?'

'Miss…' stammered Jemma. 'I didn't see what happened next.'

Miss Lauren gave her a look. A teacher's look.

'After David hit Adrian and ran away, did Adrian run after him instead of coming to get me?'

Jemma's face fell as she realised she'd been tricked and made a mess of things. Adrian glared at her. He didn't need her help! The tears welled up in her eyes. She'd been caught out telling lies. That wasn't fair. David hit Adrian from behind. She wasn't lying when she said that! Annette was her friend but Annette liked David too. That wasn't fair either! Then the tears rolled down her cheeks. David looked at her with contempt. She'd lied about him and then started crying when she was found out. But he didn't know how painful it was for Jemma. She had to share her best friend. He didn't know how a pain like that could make her bitter. But Miss Lauren did know. Her heart softened towards Jemma but she didn't want to hear any more of her lies.

'Alright, Jemma. Thank you for coming forward. That was very brave but I don't think you really saw what happened.'

Jemma stepped back, defeated. But David was still in trouble. He'd been fighting and there was no getting away from that.

'I'll have to take you to see Mr Williams. All fights have to be reported. That's the rule.' She marched

all three of them towards the main building. The playground was very dull and lifeless. It made her feel so uneasy.

'Oh, has there been a fight?' asked Mrs GwraK. She was standing in front of the main doors to the school. Clinging to her leg, and taking comfort from her hand on his shoulder, was Graham.

'What are you doing with that boy?' demanded Miss Lauren.

'I've been comforting him,' replied Mrs GwraK smoothly. 'He was very upset.'

Miss Lauren rushed towards the boy. She bent down and looked into his eyes. They were dull and glassy. He smiled stupidly at her.

'She's a lovely lady,' he said thickly. 'I like her a lot.'

Miss Lauren stood up straight. Now she really was angry. Just about as angry as she could be. David knew her anger, but not this rage building up inside her. Her fists were clenched and her shoulders taught. Hide it! Hide your anger from her! Hide it or she'll get you! But it was no use. Miss Lauren's eyes were blazing and she was ready to confront Mrs GwraK.

'Has there been a fight?' Mrs GwraK asked again.

'Yes there has,' said Miss Lauren sternly, her jaw clenched with suppressed fury. 'And this other one is ill.'

'Oh I am sorry to hear that. I hope it's nothing to

do with the food.' She smiled her big, wide smile but as always it only made her eyes cold and nasty.

Miss Lauren faced Mrs GwraK and David knew she was furious enough to let rip. She would tell her everything in her anger. And then Mrs GwraK would know who her enemies were. She would secretly destroy Miss Lauren and David would be all alone to fight against the witch. He knew that. He knew that by instinct!

Just as Miss Lauren was about to speak, David trod on her foot as if by accident. She turned on him but saw the pleading look in his eyes.

He whispered to her: 'Don't tell her about me! Don't!'

Miss Lauren kept silent but Mrs GwraK released Graham and looked down at David.

'Haven't I seen you before?' she asked in her sweetest voice. 'You were outside the headteacher's office yesterday. And now you've been fighting.' She ruffled his hair and he felt the knobbly joints of her fingers on his scalp and tried not to wince.

'What is your name?' David looked at the ground.

'David Roberts,' he said quietly.

'Ah, David Roberts. I'll remember that.'

Then he felt Miss Lauren jerk him away from her.

'I'll take them to see Mr Williams,' she said firmly.

'And the boy who's ill?' asked Mrs GwraK kindly. 'Would you like me to take care of him?'

'No thank you,' said Miss Lauren sharply.

David glanced back as Miss Lauren took them into the school. Mrs GwraK was watching them go. What did she want? What was she planning? David didn't know. But the last thing you ever wanted was for a witch to notice you and ask your name.

bad name

David and Adrian stood outside Mr Williams' office as Miss Lauren took Gareth in. Now David had time to think.

Mrs GwraK had noticed him and that was bad. From now on he must be just normal and blend in with the other children. No more fights or rows or anything to make him stand out. He had Miss Lauren on his side and she wasn't going to eat any of the food either. Then it dawned on him: maybe a teacher could get away with not eating the food, but he couldn't. He was just a kid. Mrs GwraK would notice and she would do something about it. He had to secretly get rid of the food somehow.

'Adrian?' he whispered.

'Uh?' Adrian glowered at him.

'You can have all my food from now on. I don't want it. It's disgusting.'

Adrian just didn't understand David at all. How could he say the food was disgusting? It was the most delicious Golden Food! But if David didn't like it, Adrian was more than happy to have a double share. He sneered at him for being such an idiot.

'One thing, though,' added David. 'You'll have to keep quiet about it. No boasting or gloating or a lot of other kids are going to want a share.'

'I'll handle them.'

'You could handle them but they'll soon tell tales about it. And the teachers will put a stop to it.'

Adrian hadn't thought of that. He gritted his teeth. The very thought of David being right was like a fire on his skin. But he wanted that food.

'If that's the way you want it,' he sneered.

'There's something else. You'll have to take the blame for the fight.'

'No way!' hissed Adrian. 'You hit me from behind.'

'You'll take the blame,' insisted David, 'and pretend we're friends.'

'What?!' stammered Adrian. That fire on his skin flared into an inferno.

'Look. If Mr Williams thinks we're enemies…'

'We are enemies.'

'Yeah, alright. We are enemies. But if they know we're enemies they won't let us sit next to each other at lunchtime. How will you get your food then, Adrian?'

This was too much for Adrian. That inferno consumed him now but any pain was worth it for extra portions of the Golden Food.

'Yeah, okay,' he said as if he didn't care. 'If that's what makes you happy.'

The office door opened and Gareth stepped out, smiling and full of life; followed by a very annoyed Mr Williams and a puzzled Miss Lauren.

'I just don't understand it,' said Miss Lauren. 'Five minutes ago he was in a daze!'

'He seems lively enough to me,' retorted Mr Williams.

'But the whole playground is so quiet and dull.'

They all listened to the sounds of the playground outside. All of a sudden there was laughter, shouting and delighted screams of playing. Nothing dull at all. Two of the younger children came crashing in through the main door, laughing as they chased each other. They stopped when they saw Mr Williams and Miss Lauren. They straightened themselves up and darted back out again before they got a row for running. Mr Williams gave Miss Lauren a stern look. And that was only the start. That purple colour had invaded his face and nothing on earth could stop his tiny little mind from getting angry. He was going to give a row.

'Miss Lauren, I find your attitude abnormal. You march a boy into my room, claiming he is ill because of the new and delicious food. Then you launch into a diatribe against the new cook even though the previous cook, Mrs Jones, about whom you have made no complaint, put such a collection of insects and vermin of every description in the food of our children that we were all ill for a week. We're lucky anyone can still eat anything after that. Are you saying Mrs Jones did nothing wrong?'

'I didn't say that,' protested Miss Lauren.

'No but you meant to say it. I heard you.'

'You heard me say what I meant?' She was starting to get confused.

'Didn't you mean what you said?' he retorted.

'Yes, I meant what I said.'

'Then you did say it. I thought so.' His finger jabbed at her in triumph.

'Did you say you heard what you thought I said?' she asked. This was getting beyond her.

'Are you saying I didn't hear you?'

'No. But what you thought you heard wasn't what I said.'

'Ah-ha!' Mr Williams had a demented gleam of satisfaction in his eye. 'Now I've caught you talking drivel! Pure drivel! What you thought you meant to say isn't what you meant when you said what you did say! Is that what you said? Is that what you meant to say or is there some other meaning that I only thought I hadn't thought of? I mean, Miss Lauren. Be careful! For the first time ever, a healthy diet and a taste experience have been combined in one. I am in a state of ecstatic delight. Every teacher except you is likewise ecstatic. And the children also. Always think of the children! They loved the food. We all loved it. We were delighted. We were in a state of sated satisfaction before you came bursting in to disturb our slee…' Mr Williams stopped himself just in time. 'My… my well deserved repose. I'll say this once and you will take heed. I will not tolerate sniping criticisms of Mrs GwraK and her wonderful food.'

He looked down at Gareth. He didn't want to be bothered by useless children.

'Right, Gareth. You can go.' Gareth didn't know what was going on. He gave David a questioning look but Mr Williams had told him to go. Adrian stepped forward.

'Please, Sir,' he said like a little angel. 'It was all my fault.'

Miss Lauren stared at him in amazement: 'Sir? Please, Sir? It was all my fault?' She'd never ever heard Adrian talk like that. She didn't even know he *could* talk like that. Something was up and she knew it. They'd invented a story to tell and she was going to get to the bottom of it.

But Mr Williams was thrilled. He'd never seen or heard anything like it either. A boy! A boy had stepped forward and taken the blame! And he'd said sorry with honour.

'Do you admit that you were fighting?' he asked.

'Yes.'

'And do you realise that it's bad to fight?'

'Yes.'

'And do you also take the blame for fighting?'

'Yes,' Adrian looked Mr Williams straight in the eye.

Mr Williams turned on David.

'You see?' he thundered. 'You could learn from this boy!' He put his hand on Adrian's shoulder. 'You were both fighting but he admits it.'

David hadn't opened his mouth.

'He doesn't fight and then tell lies about it. And it's the lies I can't stand! Boys will be boys but lies are lies!'

Lies? David hadn't lied! He hadn't been given a chance to tell his lies! Adrian put on an even more angelic look.

'Please, Sir, don't blame David. It was a fair fight and I was to blame.'

Mr Williams almost fainted with delight. He loved the honesty of this boy.

'We're good friends, really. But our play-fighting got a bit out of hand.' Then he turned towards David.

'I'm sorry I lost my temper, David.' He thrust out his hand for David to shake but David was so surprised, he couldn't react. He just stood there in shock, looking at Adrian.

'How dare you refuse to shake hands with this boy!' thundered Mr Williams. Miss Lauren tried to speak but he shushed her.

'No, no Miss Lauren! This is the second time this week I've had to tell this boy.' Then he turned back to David. 'You are a lazy, daydreaming, fighting, cowardly liar and I won't stand for it in my school! Do you hear me?'

'Yes, Sir,' said David even though the accusation

was so unfair. Miss Lauren glared at Mr Williams but he turned on her. 'This is how you get at the truth, Miss Lauren. Listen and learn.' Then he turned back to David. 'I'm going to write a letter to your parents and you're going to deliver it yourself! Now get back to your class. Lunchtime is over!' He went back into his office, slamming the door behind him.

'David, I need a quiet word with you alone.' They were in the classroom but the other kids hadn't come back in from the yard.

'I'm very, very…' she searched for the right word. 'I'm very concerned.'

David had waited for her to say something big – that she was frightened, angry, terrified, determined to fight. Ready to die to rid the world of the witch. And out popped that wimp word, concerned. He hated that word – he'd heard it so many times. It was a false word used by adults to dodge the truth. It was like that other word he hated and never really understood. He didn't even know how to spell it. In-app-rop-ri-ate. They were always using that word against him. Always! But it was so empty. A nothing word. An adult word that could catch any crime. 'That's in-app-rop-ri-ate behaviour, David', they'd tell him but they'd never explain what was actually wrong. 'David, doing that is in-app-rop-ri-ate' they'd say and inside his head his brain would scream 'Tell me exactly what is wrong!' but they never did. They just used the magic word and expected him to obey. He hoped Miss Lauren wasn't going to say something stupid like: 'It's in-app-rop-ri-ate for a witch to be the school cook.' That would just do his head in. He needed something stronger than that. Much, much stronger.

'She's a witch, Miss Lauren! A real witch! And she's got Mr Williams wrapped round her little finger. We've got to do something.'

Miss Lauren stared at him, shocked by his directness. Then her shoulders collapsed and she heaved a great sigh as she let her fear show.

'I'm a teacher. I'm not supposed to believe in things like that. Things like that aren't supposed to be true.'

'She's a witch. We both know it. We might as well admit it or it'll be too late.'

'I know. I know she's a witch but I don't know what to do!'

Just then, the other kids came lumbering in and Miss Lauren put on her teacher's face. She seemed perfectly normal but David could see the strain behind the eyes.

'Everybody sit down. I have your projects to give back to you,' said Miss Lauren. Then she whispered. 'Go to your seat now, David. We'll talk later. When I've had time to think.'

David felt a sense of relief as he went to his seat. At last he had an adult who could see the truth. He wasn't alone anymore and wouldn't have to fight the witch all by himself. Miss Lauren would do that. She was a good teacher and people would listen to her. And they would be a team. He wouldn't have to carry the secret alone.

Miss Lauren went about the class handing out the projects as if there was nothing wrong. David was glad. At last she'd learnt to put on an act. Pretend there was nothing to worry about. That was the only way.

'I've marked them and I really think you've all done some excellent work. You've all worked very hard.'

Miss Lauren activated the computer, turned to the interactive whiteboard and wrote out the title of the lesson. Some of the children started murmuring as they looked inside their workbooks. Without turning round, she called out: 'Silence, please!'

The murmuring just grew louder and louder. David opened his workbook and read the comment. It was written in Miss Lauren's handwriting: 'Do you call this a project, you lazy, daydreaming, useless little boy? It's rubbish and so are you.'

Miss Lauren hadn't written anything like that before. He swapped workbooks with Gareth. Written in his workbook were the words: 'You are just so stupid!'

'What does she mean by that?' asked Gareth.

Of all the children, only Adrian was happy as he read the comment: 'You miserable git! I'll get you one day, you can be sure of that.'

He liked that. It was nasty. He was the youngest

of three boys and an elder sister and that was exactly the sort of thing they said to him. From now on, he was going to like Miss Lauren.

Miss Lauren turned from the whiteboard and faced the class.

'I said that's enough!' she shouted above the noise. All the children looked up and gasped aloud. Written on the whiteboard, in large letters was a great big NAUGHTY WORD.

Some of the boys began to snigger and Miss Lauren realised something was wrong. When she turned round and saw the word she was shocked. That wasn't what she'd written! She rushed to the computer and tried to delete it but the computer had frozen. She pressed every key she could think of but the word just hung there. She tried to switch the computer off, but it wouldn't respond. What was happening? She tried to scribble the word away with the pen but that didn't work either. She began to panic. She scratched at the word with her nails even though she knew that was no use. She turned towards David and as their eyes met, they both knew. It was Mrs GwraK. She had done this.

Then, one of the girls who was always very, very good started to cry. Miss Lauren, or rather Mrs GwraK, had written in her workbook: 'You are a goody-goody telltale cry baby. You only behave well to make yourself better than everybody else but I know what you're really like.'

This sentence had upset her a lot and she had sat

there, building up her tears. She was a tyrant with her tears. She started crying and wailing and she ran out of the class to fetch Mr Williams. This was going to be great, an once-in-a-lifetime prize. She was going to tell tales on a teacher.

Mr Williams came storming into the class, the girl not far behind. By now she was in a flood of tears and her cheeks were red as if she'd suffered the very worst thing ever. It felt so right to be offended. She was at the front of the class and she was in the right. The headteacher himself had said so.

'What's come over you, Miss Lauren?' he demanded. Before she could answer he carried on: 'You go chasing frogs across the canteen with no regard for safety. Then you burst into my office to tell lies about a valued member of staff and the condition of these healthy, active and articulate children. Then you insult them with personal remarks in their workbooks and write a great big dirty word on the board. It's just not good enough!'

Miss Lauren was too aghast to respond. Chasing frogs? How dare he say that! And what frogs? It was *one* frog and he'd told her to chase it. Mr Williams turned to face the class, to reassure them that everything was alright. He had his arms outstretched ready to instil calm. But he had stepped into the beam of the projector and the naughty word was now written on his forehead. Before he could say anything the pupils burst out laughing. They were laughing at him and he was the only one who couldn't see why they were in hysterics. His blood boiled.

'Get out of my school!' he shouted at Miss Lauren.

'But Mr Williams…' she began. He shouted her down.

'No, no, Miss Lauren. When it comes to the children of this school I will brook no bad behaviour. Get out of this class! Leave the school now and never return!'

Miss Lauren made one more attempt to explain but Mr Williams shouted at her: 'I will not listen to your pathetic excuses! Get out! Get out! Get out now! You are sacked! Dismissed! You're fired! You will never teach in this or any other school again!'

For a short while Miss Lauren stood there in shock. She felt like a child being given a row for something she hadn't done. And she wasn't allowed to speak! She was so choked with emotion that she couldn't speak anyway. Her throat was tied into a knot. It felt punched from the inside. Her lower lip trembled and her eyes welled with tears. She turned to look at the children but they vanished in a glittering blur. She ran out of the room. As she reached the door, she turned to look for David. Her tears had made her blind and her eyes darted this way and that but David saw what she was trying to do. He half rose from his seat. The anger of his headteacher and the slyness of the witch meant he could do no more than that. She could not see him. She slammed the door after her, the only useless protest she could make against the injustice of it all.

Mr Williams collected the workbooks and put them in a drawer and pulled the plug on the computer. The naughty word died with a groan. He told the children that Miss Lauren was ill. No one believed him. Only David knew what had really happened and what it meant. Miss Lauren had no power now. And David was all alone.

obey

David was really hungry by the time he arrived home but he didn't want his mum to know in case she started asking questions. So when she left the kitchen, he hurriedly made himself a really untidy sandwich and scoffed it down before she came back. It wasn't the same as a meal, but he didn't want to spoil his appetite for supper. What was that witch doing? He couldn't work it out. The food had made everyone zombified. There was no feeling in that playground. No playing. Nothing. But bad feeling was alive. Anger and violence could erupt. Malice was wide awake. Jemma had proved it. She'd lied outright against him. Was that what the witch was after? To kill all good feeling and exaggerate the bad? Why would she want that? What did she want, really want? And why did she want it?

He heard the front door and he knew his dad had arrived home. He would have to show them the letter from Mr Williams. His dad rushed in and hugged his wife and spun her around the kitchen. Then he let go of her and hugged David. He was whooping for joy as he waved a letter about. David didn't understand. It couldn't be Mr Williams' letter!

'You've got the job!' shouted his mum.

'Yes!' shouted his dad. 'Yeeeeeeeeees!' And he hugged his wife again. His dad reached out to bring David into the hug but David pulled back. He didn't want to spoil his parents' happiness with his bad news.

'What's the matter, David?' asked his dad.

'Is anything wrong?' asked his mum.

'Why the long face?' said his dad. 'With this new job we've got more money. We can have better holidays. More presents at Christmas.'

That only made it worse. His dad had been worried for ages about getting this new job and David knew how unhappy his parents had been because they didn't have enough money. Now they were happy because his dad had got the job and things could get better for them at last. But David was spoiling their happiness and he pulled away from them. There was a witch in the school! She was poisoning the children and only David knew it! He pulled out the letter and showed it to them. How could he explain? They'd think he was mad!

'I'm sorry! I'm sorry!' was all he could say.

Later that night, David was sitting up in bed with his games console. He couldn't get into it. He got killed in minutes by enemies he'd always found easy to defeat before and he couldn't be bothered getting to the next level. His dad came in and sat on the edge of the bed.

'Look,' he began. 'We know what Adrian's like. I don't care what anybody says, he's never been anything but trouble. If you fought with him, he started it. We know that.'

'He was beating up Gareth.'

'Yes, you told us. Mr Williams doesn't expect us to go see him. This letter is just to warn us that there may be problems. But you're a normal boy. We know that too.' He put his arm around David and pulled his head onto his chest.

David had to say something. He needed help and maybe his dad would believe him.

'Dad? Do witches really exist?'

'No. Not really.'

'What if I said I've seen a witch. A real one.'

'Ha! How would you know she was a witch? She would have a disguise. She would be plotting and waiting for the best moment to strike. Normally a witch would appear to be a kindly old lady. And she'd have an apple. A shiny, deep red apple. A poisoned apple that looked delicious. She'd get you to eat it and, Blam!'

'Blam what?!' demanded David, his mouth agape.

'Blam bam, all of a sudden she puts you under her spell or she might just put you in her cauldron.' He grinned at his son, sucked his lips over his teeth and gave a cackling laugh. 'Don't forget the laugh' he said in a cartoon witch voice. 'He, he, he, heeeeeee!'

'But dad, I have seen a witch. I can see through

her disguise. And so could Miss Lauren. That's why the witch made her look silly – so no one would believe her. She made her look bad.'

His dad pulled away from him. He looked strangely at David and said: 'Do you believe that?'

'Yes.'

'David, I think you need help.'

'Will you help me?'

'Yes, David. I'm sorry but I am going to have to help you. This daydreaming has gone too far.'

The doctor arrived that same night. He was a jolly man, older than David's parents and with a loud, booming voice. David knew why the doctor was there – his parents thought he had gone mad. They thought Mrs Jones was mad and they thought Miss Lauren was mad. That's how the witch destroyed her enemies. She made people think they were mad.

'Hello, hello,' said the doctor as he entered the bedroom. David's parents stayed by the doorway. His mother was grabbing on to his father's arm and trying not to cry.

'Your name is David,' said the doctor. 'Am I right?'

'Yes.'

'Good, good. Now, I hear you've been getting some strange ideas.'

How could he answer that? The doctor wouldn't

believe him. No one would. He sat on the edge of the bed.

'Believe it or not, it's normal to have strange ideas.' David stayed silent so the doctor turned to his parents. 'Perhaps I could speak to him alone.'

His mum and dad went quietly downstairs. The doctor took out a medical torch with a small, powerful beam. He switched it on and looked into David's eyes. Then, slowly at first, he swayed it smoothly from side to side, backwards and forwards, side to side. David started to feel sleepy. The doctor swung the torch faster and faster and hissed like a rasping snake:

'I am a servant of the witch! Obey her command and eat the food!'

the·good·Mrs.Gwrak

David's parents kept him home from school for a day or two to get better. He was very pale but his parents were glad he'd stopped believing he'd seen a witch. They thought the doctor was marvellous.

But the time had come for him to return to school and he was looking forward to it. As he walked through the school gates he saw that in just a few days all the children had grown enormously fat. But it wasn't a natural fat. This fat was like an extra layer beneath the skin; an unnatural padding that stretched the skin taut. David now wanted to be like them and he was really looking forward to the food.

Gareth came bounding up to him. He was the only lively kid in the playground and David soon found out why.

'Am I getting your food today?' he asked eagerly, his eyes glittering.

'No,' said David flatly. 'I want it.'

'No you don't! You hate it!'

'Not any more. I love the food now.'

Gareth glared at him and shouted at the top of his voice: 'No you don't! You're a liar! You don't like the food and you should give it to me! You should give me your food! That's what a real friend would do!'

David could see some of the children turn to stare at him. Gareth saw them as well.

'He doesn't like the Golden Food!' he shouted, pointing at David. There was a gasp of amazement and David saw their eyes light up. He could sense their greed. He doesn't like the food. He'll have some food to give us. Extra food. More Golden Food. He can give us more. Some of the children started inching closer and more children were joining them from the playing field, attracted by Gareth's protests. They circled round David and pressed closer and closer. 'Golden Food! Golden Food! He doesn't like his Golden Food!' David felt their weight pressing against him. And suddenly he felt the danger he was in. They were squashing the breath out of him! He couldn't breathe. There was no escape as more and more children joined in. Soon, the entire school had joined in. They all pressed and pushed to get at David. He was being crushed.

One of them called out: 'If you don't like the food, you should share it.'

'Yes,' called out another kid who David didn't even know. 'Share it with me! I'm your friend!'

As David felt the last of his breath forced out of him, the pleading began.

'Can I have some?'

'No! Give me some! Pleeeeeease!'

'Pleeeeeeeeeeease!'

They pressed closer and closer: pawing at him, grabbing at him and begging for his share of the Golden Food. They tugged at his clothes and hair. He felt their hands grabbing at him, pulling his skin in a desperate attempt to get his attention. They were clawing at him, their fingers digging into his flesh. And all the while, the crushing got much worse.

Suddenly, the grabbing and the pleading stopped. David felt the pressure ease as the crowd dispersed and he fell to his knees, gulping for air. He looked up as a dark shadow fell on him. It was Mrs GwraK.

'Thank you,' said David. 'You saved my life.'

The witch smiled down at him. She helped him to his feet and when she ruffled his hair with her knobbly fingers, he loved it.

At lunchtime, David queued for his Golden Food. The smell was delicious and he couldn't understand why he'd hated it before. It made his head spin with pleasure and he could only imagine the taste of it melting on his tongue. At last he reached the serving hatch and Mrs GwraK smiled down at him again.

'You deserve a double portion.'

David was thrilled. 'Thank you again,' he said eagerly.

As she leaned over to give him his double portion, thick globules of spit dribbled down from her warty mouth and onto the plate. They glistened and glinted and dripped down to mix with the nasty fat. David was even more thrilled. A double portion of the most delicious food ever! A double portion of Golden Food, served in a gravy of her own spit! All the other children scowled at him with envy. It wasn't fair! He didn't deserve a double share! Even Mr Williams, sitting at his table and waiting to be

served, saw the treat David was getting. His face flushed with indignation. That David was nothing but trouble.

When David sat down at his table Jemma smiled sweetly at him, hoping to get a share of his food. Adrian sneered at him for a second, before wolfing down his own miserable single portion. All the children were wolfing down their food. All except David. He had a double portion and he was going to savour it slowly, rolling it around his tongue and chewing all the fatty flavour out of it. He brought a forkful of it up to his drooling lips. The golden smell made him light-headed. But, as it plopped into his mouth, the real rancid taste made his tongue shrivel. The ugly taste of a dead, wet rat was in his mouth, and he swallowed it.

As the food slid down to his stomach, the grease congealed into a heavy lump that fizzled and bubbled like acid. It was like eating a ball of twisted needles. His knotted guts clung to the food even as it stung and pierced him from inside. His head swam and he felt dazed, but it was also as if he was waking up. Now he remembered the words of the doctor: 'I am a servant of the witch! Obey her command and eat the food!' He had been hypnotised.

With a feeling of disgust he remembered adoring and thanking Mrs GwraK. Then he remembered how she really was and he saw her real self. Her skin was a pale grey with a green tinge, her face was a plague of warts and her mouth had only a few stumpy, yellow teeth and a coarse tongue. He remembered her spit dribbling down her tongue and onto his food. Now the spell was broken sickness rose up and clutched at his throat. No. He mustn't be sick. He mustn't! He knew Mrs GwraK must be watching him. He fought against it but he knew he couldn't ever eat another morsel of that filth.

Everyone had their heads down, their mouths racing through the food. Mr Williams had lost all control. He was grabbing huge chunks of the food with his hands and stuffing them into his wide open mouth. His eyes glistened with delight as he chewed. He smacked his lips and rolled his tongue around his mouth.

'Isn't she marvellous?' he exclaimed to the other teachers. 'Isn't she just the most marvellous cook ever? Eh?'

The other teachers nodded their agreement as they too stuffed their faces full of the food. David copied their actions without really eating anything. He slid his elbow along the table and nudged Adrian who darted a threatening look at him. But he smiled greedily when he saw what David was offering. He was using his arm as cover to slide his double-full plate towards him. Adrian slid his own empty plate to David. The swap was swiftly made and David carried on pretending to gorge himself on the food.

Adrian couldn't believe his luck. He'd bullied and threatened and fought for only one extra portion, and he was having double. That made three full portions of Golden Food. A lot more than anyone else. Even more than Gareth!

Jemma finished her plate and looked up. Her brows knitted suspiciously. How come Adrian had so much food left to eat and David had finished his? David put a dazed look on his face as Jemma eyed them both. Had they swapped plates? She would tell Mrs GwraK if they had. But Jemma hadn't seen the swap and if David had eaten two portions and Jemma told Mrs GwraK that he hadn't, he would get a third portion absolutely free! Huh! No way. No. She wasn't going to hand him a third portion when she'd only had one. David sat back in his chair.

'Ah,' he said to Jemma, rubbing his belly. 'Double portions.'

'You don't deserve double portions!' she spat at him.

'Never mind deserving it. I got double portions and that's what counts.'

David saw Mrs GwraK looking at him. She smiled. He smiled back, with a dazed and stupid look on his face. Yes! He'd fooled the witch! And he'd keep on fooling her. It was Friday. That gave him the weekend to work out a plan. He needed to do more than just fool her. He was going to destroy her. Whatever plan she had, his plan would be better and he would put an end to her.

After lunch, David went looking for Annette. She was always so very sensible and he wanted to know what she thought of the new cook. He found her at the far end of the yard but she'd grown just as fat as all the other children. David was shocked at the sight of her.

'Annette?' he asked.

'Hello, David,' she replied. 'Are you feeling better?'

'Yes. But what about you? Have you been eating the food?'

'Of course I have.'

'But I thought you didn't like it.'

'I didn't at first and I was going to complain but Mrs GwraK came over to my house and explained everything.'

'She came over to your house?'

'Yes. And now I like the food. She told my parents it was very important that I should eat the food and I agree with her.'

David backed away.

'Have you been eating the food?' she asked. 'You don't look healthy at all. You're far too skinny.'

'I've just had a double portion,' he lied.

'That's good. You're always causing trouble. That's your problem and I do worry about you.'

'There's no need to worry.'

'No. Not if you're eating the food. Mrs GwraK said

that if I complained about the food it would cause a lot of trouble. I didn't want to do that.'

'I suppose not,' said David, still backing away. The witch had turned Annette against herself, using her sensible nature to silence her complaints. He couldn't stand it any more. They'd always been friends and to see her so changed was too much. As he walked away, she called out after him.

'She's gone to a lot of trouble to make that nutritious food. She's worked very hard. It would be wrong not to eat it after all her hard work.'

David was already too far away and couldn't hear her.

He saw Adrian sitting on the school wall, leaning back against the railings. He was just sitting there, out of breath and puffing. In less than half an hour that floppy padding of fat had grown and his skin was stretched so tight it was shining. His belly flopped out beneath his shirt and his neck was as thick as his head. He had a huge, almost solid double chin and his mouth hung open. Spit dribbled down from it in a stream. It was the three portions that had done that to him and David felt guilty. But what could he do? Soon, everyone would be just like Adrian – too out of breath to move and too dazed to think. And David really would stand out if he wasn't eating the food. He needed to get away from Adrian. He needed to think.

As he passed the school gates he saw a policeman

leaning on the bonnet of his car. He had a clipboard in one hand and an apple in the other.

'Are you David Roberts?' he asked.

After his experience with the doctor David knew the witch had agents all about but he couldn't just ignore a policeman. He turned to face him and saw him bite into the apple. The moment he saw it, he was reminded of what his dad had said about the witch. It was an odd shaped apple, gnarled and ugly with rough brown patches all over it. And far from being a deep shiny red, it was a vibrant green with only a few patches of an earthy reddish colour. The policeman noticed David staring.

'I've just had my lunch. This is my pudding. I hope you don't mind. I wouldn't be eating it if I thought you were a criminal. I just need a word with you.'

'Where did you get the apple?' David asked. The policeman grinned.

'Not that it's any of your business, but I have an apple tree at home.'

'Why is it that funny shape?'

'I thought I was going to ask the questions.' He paused to consider. 'This apple is natural. You see these brown marks?'

'Yes.'

'It's where the leaves have rubbed against it and left a scar. Only the best apples have that, the ones that grow on the outside of the tree. They get more sun. It's the same with oranges but I don't have an orange tree.'

The policeman was very friendly. He might be able to trust him after all. He held out his hand to David.

'I'm Police Constable Bryant,' he said. 'I'm glad I found you so easily.'

'Oh?' said David. What else could he say? Bryant opened the gate and stepped into the yard. Then he closed the gate and leaned on it. 'Have I done something wrong?' asked David.

'Are you the one who was fighting the other day?'

David's heart sank. Wouldn't he ever hear the last of it? 'I had to fight. I was saving a friend,' he explained.

Bryant nodded his head. 'I thought it might be something like that. Mr Williams had to call me in. That's the way it is these days. But I don't think there's any real problem. Are you and Adrian friends now?'

David didn't like to lie but there was a lot at stake. 'Yes, we're friends.'

'Huh!' said Bryant, smiling. 'And have you shaken hands?'

'We're sort of friends,' he said after a long pause. Bryant stared at David for a while, not harshly but with concern.

'Right,' he said finally. 'There's only one problem here. You're lying to me. I don't know why, but there's something you're not telling me. And there's something wrong with this school. What's wrong with all these kids? Why are they half asleep?'

Could David trust this policeman? Could he tell him the truth?

'I don't know,' he mumbled. The policeman considered again. David didn't like the way he did that. He couldn't tell what the policeman was thinking. But the police were trained to act like that or else criminals would have an easy life.

'It must be a bit of a shock to have a policeman ask you questions,' said Bryant.

David nodded.

'But don't worry,' he continued. 'It's just a matter of routine. Just in case you're a troublemaker. Are you a troublemaker?'

'No.'

'Good,' said Bryant, but as he turned to go, he looked again at the kids in the yard. David could tell he was puzzled. Then he gave David a small card with his name and phone number. 'If there's anything to worry about, give me a call. Or if you feel I should know something – just let me know.' He got into his police car and drove away.

David felt happy for the first time since Miss Lauren was thrown out of the school. He felt there was someone he could turn to. If only he could find evidence to show Bryant, he might have a chance after all.

Nervously, David knocked on Mrs Jones' door. It was Saturday morning and David hoped she was in. He was certain it was the witch who'd put the creatures in the food to get rid of Mrs Jones and take her place. She was a grown-up and she might know how to deal with Mrs GwraK.

Mrs Jones flung open the door. Her hair was a tangled mess and her eyes were wild with fear. They darted this way and that when she saw David. Then she cupped his cheeks in her hands and looked down at him.

'Is that David Roberts?' Her voice was weak and frail.

'Yes,' he answered.

'And are you alright?'

'No!' he cried out. 'There's a witch in the school and nobody believes it!'

Suddenly, her eyes grew wide and she slammed the door in his face. For a moment David was stunned. Then he opened the letterbox and shouted: 'Please, Mrs Jones! Please! There's a witch in the school and she's going to poison us all!'

He looked through the slit of the letterbox. Mrs Jones was clinging to the banisters, looking wilder than ever before.

'Is this a trap? Are you here to trap me?'

'No! I need help! Please help me!' cried David. 'I don't know what to do. There's a policeman who might help but I don't know how to make him believe me!'

Mrs Jones let go of the banisters and stood up straight. She was trembling with fear but she came closer.

'I'm sorry to see you like this,' said David, tears brimming in his eyes. 'But please help me.'

'I can't,' she wailed. 'I can't!'

'We're being poisoned,' he pleaded.

Hopeless tears welled up in her eyes. Then she cried out: 'Evil has a smiling face and the poison is sweet. Sweet poison is the worst! It makes you want to eat it!'

She stared back at him through the letterbox. 'What is the point of a bitter poison? You won't take it! Sweet poison. Easy, greasy, melting, golden poison; a savoury sweetness greater than honey! Vile and deadly. It makes you want to eat it!'

'Will you help me?' asked David eagerly, but the hopeless look came back into her eyes.

'Go now,' she cried wildly. 'I can't help you. I am nobody and I can't help you!' She ran up the stairs to hide away from him.

'Mrs Jones!' he cried out to her. 'Come back, please! I need your help!'

But it was no use. If only he knew where Miss Lauren lived. She would help.

Then David had an idea.

David typed the word 'witch' and clicked 'search'. He was using the computer in the library in case the witch found out he was searching for her on the internet. He looked at the screen and saw there were millions of pages about witchcraft. He couldn't look at them all. He had to narrow down his search. What was her name? Mrs GwraK. He typed it in and only five choices appeared on the screen. The first two were foreign websites. David didn't understand them at all, but the third was plain enough. It said www.slaythewitch.co.uk. He clicked on the site and read the stark warning:

Beware the power of the witch

Those whom the witch wishes to destroy, she first makes mad. It is the madness of a sweet poison. So beware the witch, for her time is now and she has the twisted wisdom of her ancient evil.

Beneath the warning he saw an ancient painting of a witch. It was Mrs GwraK alright, but it wasn't exactly the same as her and it wasn't the sweet old lady he'd seen on the CCTV monitor. She had a mocking, contemptuous sneer and her eyes were full of cold, hard hatred but she didn't have any warts. She was almost handsome. The painting looked very old. Perhaps this was what she used to look like years ago. But one thing was certain – he'd found what he was looking for. He searched through the site.

You are in danger. Be careful, for the witch directs her magic with her hands and can hypnotise with her eyes. Hide from her. Do not let her know you suspect she is a witch or she will destroy you. The only way is to destroy her first, to slay her with a magic spell. You must find the lair of the witch, for it is only there and nowhere else that a certain plant grows. Its name is witchweed, and you will know it by its dark green pentagonal leaves. This plant is loathsome to the witch, for it grows beneath her feet, choking her and forcing her to move on. Only this plant can destroy the witch.

With a sprig of witchweed held aloft in your right hand you must confront the witch and recite this ancient spell.

Yn·drech·na·grym·ac·hud·y·Wrach — a·thrwy

hyn·ei·throi'n·gawlach,

yn·llwch·dyma·swyn·holl·iach

fel·saeth·i·falu·sothach.

He wrote it down on a piece of paper. This was good, he thought. The internet was full of ancient knowledge.

This will rob her of all her power. Once this is done, you must approach the witch and touch her with the sprig of witchweed. At that very moment the witch will turn to dust. Lay the sprig on the pile of dust and wait for the wind to scatter her to nothing. There must be no witnesses or else the witch may transfer her spirit.

But where was her lair? He scrolled down the page and that's when he saw the photograph. David swallowed hard. It was the old mansion house. It had been empty for years and years but the witch must be living there now.

'That's where I'll get some witchweed,' he said out loud. One of the librarians turned to look at him. David kept his head down. He mustn't attract attention. He couldn't trust anyone, not even a librarian.

He would have to get some witchweed, confront the witch alone and recite this strange spell. If he failed then that would be the end of him, and a terrible fate would befall the school and all the children in it.

the·lair·of·the·Witch

When night fell and his parents went to bed, David got up and dressed in his darkest, blackest clothes. He put his torch in his pocket and sneaked out of the house.

The night was cold and empty and the moon was blotted out by a thick bank of clouds. He had to use his torch. He had hoped to save the batteries for when he reached the witch's house, in case they ran out.

It was a long walk to the derelict old mansion and, as he got nearer, he found it more and more difficult to move his feet forward. He'd gone past that derelict old mansion many times in the car and he'd always thought it was haunted. His dad always slowed down a little bit to prolong the agony and David would beg him to drive on, to get away from the house as quickly as possible. Everyone called it the haunted house and even the toughest boys, or the biggest boasters, admitted they were too terrified to go near the place, in case they were forced to prove how brave they were.

His mum always reassured him it wasn't haunted; that there weren't any such things as ghosts. He'd always felt that was just his mum trying to make him feel better, and he'd needed that, especially with his dad slowing down and giggling. But you couldn't tell a child there were no such things as ghosts; not when you looked at that broken down old house. Not even in broad daylight. And now it was dead of night. He was terrified and more than anything he wanted to turn and run or sneak away and hide. No! He had to go on.

At last he saw the high stone wall that surrounded the house and grounds. It was much taller than him. He switched his torch off and at that moment the thick clouds drifted on, revealing a gleaming full moon. The landscape was transformed from pure, empty black into dark blue with stark highlights of white and deep pools of ominous black shadow. He could see the huge wall clearly now and he remembered that further along there was a large gateway with vast pillars and gates of snarled and twisted wrought iron. He would have to be careful. The witch could be out and about at night and David didn't know if she could see in the dark. The thought shivered through his body as his terror grew. But the terror also made him think. Near the gates would be the most dangerous place. He might be able to sneak a look but he couldn't go through.

He made his way along the grey stone wall, reached the gate pillar and peered into the grounds. It was a forbidding place. The mansion seemed to be crumbling and sinking into the ground. Its roof was jagged and many of its slates had fallen. The windows had no glass and the frames had long since rotted away leaving three gaping holes that seemed to snarl like the mouths of angry, screaming ghouls. A huge crack ran along the front of the mansion and it was a miracle that the building was still standing. This crack was crooked like an evil smile and it seemed to David that the rubble piled on the floor had been vomited by the mansion through this otherwise devouring mouth.

The grounds were overgrown and rank with weeds. Huge trees surrounded the back and sides of the mansion and the derelict roofs of outbuildings and stables showed through the canopy. David didn't even want to think about venturing into those dark woods.

But what really caught his attention was the witchweed. It grew like a thick carpet through the long grass, on the gravel of the drive and up the walls of the terraces. Some of it was almost within reach. David stretched out on the cold damp ground as close to the pillar as he could, keeping low and moving slowly. He inched his hand forward, then his body, until at last his head was pressed against the iron gates. A clump of witchweed was only inches from his grasp. He pushed himself forward but his head was squeezed hard between the gate and the ground. With less than an inch between him and the clump of witchweed, he made one last frantic stretch, but the plant remained tantalisingly out of reach.

David lay there for a few seconds, breathing heavily. Then a light appeared in an upstairs window and he caught sight of the witch. She was standing at the window with an evil-looking lantern in her hand: a skull with a black candle alight inside it. She was staring out. Was she staring at him? What was she up to? He could see her because of the light in the room but he wasn't sure whether she could see him. He didn't dare move as the witch stretched out her arms and closed the ragged curtains. With the curtains closed, he crept away from the gate. Then, quicker than was humanly possible, she appeared at another window and stared out again. David was sure she was looking directly at the gates. She *must* have seen him in the moonlight. She seemed to be gazing straight at him with those cold, grey, piercing eyes glinting in the flickering beam of her lantern. His heart thumped punch after punch, but he didn't dare move.

He heard the rumbling of a lorry in the distance. It was coming closer along the road. The witch heard it too and her head twitched slightly towards the noise.

'Get away from the window!' he muttered desperately.

If the witch stayed where she was then David would be caught in the glare of the lorry's headlights. The driver would see him too. He might even stop to see what he was doing there. That would really catch the attention of the witch. She would come out in her disguise of a kindly old lady and he would be caught. She would volunteer to take the poor boy indoors and look after him and the driver would approve. He might even help and thank her for taking the trouble. The witch would drag him through those rotted front doors and into the snarling jaws of the mansion and he would never be seen again.

The top of the pillars were bright in the glare of

the approaching headlights, showing every stone and every crack in the cement. As the vehicle came nearer, the lights swept down the pillars, but still the witch stayed at the window. The rumbling got louder and louder as the lights grew brighter and brighter. Soon, David would be caught in their beam and that would be the end of him. The witch withdrew her lantern and twitched the curtains closed. He saw her shadow move away. He rolled to one side and dived into the ditch just as the lorry swept by and, with brakes squealing, stopped at the gates. Had the driver seen him? David kept as still as he could. The driver tooted his horn and climbed out of the cab – the noisy, rattling engine idling and belching out thick poisonous fumes. They caught in David's throat and made him want to cough. But even with the sound of the engine, he didn't dare move an inch in case he was heard.

After a while there were footsteps on the gravel and the clunking sound of the gates being opened. Their hinges creaked and squealed, first one, then the other.

'You're late,' said the witch. David looked up and saw that she was standing only four feet away from him. A slight turn of her head and she would see him for certain.

'I'm so very, very sorry,' grovelled the driver. 'It couldn't be helped.'

The witch gave him a look of withering contempt and he shrivelled before her.

'I've planned and schemed and waited long enough without you spoiling things. This is the last delivery. Drive it to the usual place.'

The driver scuttled back into the cab and revved the engine. A great black cloud of dirty fumes shot out of the exhaust straight at David. He held his nose and clasped his hand to his mouth. A choking cough caught at his throat, itching and burning. He swallowed hard to stop it but the need to cough grew and grew as the lorry roared on through the gates and the witch stepped aside to let it pass. Now she was only two feet away from him as he strained against the burning cough. She must sense his presence! Any second now she would turn around and stare right back at him.

But all she did was wait for the lorry to go through the gates and close them. He heard her retreating steps along the gravel path and a muttered curse towards the witchweed beneath her feet. After a long while he felt it was safe. He pressed both hands against his mouth and hacked a dry, scorching cough that scraped the inside of his throat. Again and again he coughed until the itch was scratched away by the blasts of air and spit. By the end of it, he was on his knees and fighting for breath.

It was a long time before he could bring himself to move and climb out of the ditch. His throat was on fire and he felt ill, exhausted, cold, wet and sad. His courage was shredded to a mangled pulp. Her voice – that rasping, lacerating voice had been too much for him. He hadn't got a sprig of the witchweed. He was defeated and he had no choice but to go home. By the light of the moon, he made his way along the road.

He hated the feeling of failure, but he was beaten. The witch was too strong for him, too fearsome. His spirit was broken. She had won.

He reached the corner of the high wall and stopped. If he walked on further, that would be the end. He tried to remember his anger; to feel it again, to be angry enough to turn around and go after the witch. But fear and despair seeped into his bones and made him feel hollow inside. That stopped him. That hollow despair was too unbearable. He turned and looked again at the wall. Before he had time to think, he was scrambling along the side, furiously making his way towards the back of the mansion to find a place where he could climb over.

He fumbled about and bumped into a tree. He didn't dare risk using his torch. Looking up, he saw that its thick branches were growing against the top of the wall. He felt along the trunk and started to climb. With only a little effort he soon reached the top of the wall and stood on it, using the branches to keep his balance. The woods and undergrowth below were in complete darkness but he climbed onto the largest branch. It curved downwards into the darkness. Under his weight, it bent low enough for him to reach the ground.

It was a strange feeling to stand on the witch's land.

It made him tingle with fear. He let go of the branch and it sprang back only slightly. He could easily reach up for it again when he needed to escape.

He set to work, still listening for any sign of the witch. He grabbed clumps of weeds and grass and ripped them out before holding them up against the light of the moon. He was looking for the telltale shape of the leaves. Again and again he tore clumps from the ground to examine them, but he never saw any sign of the witchweed. He had to go deeper into the woods. The deep black, darker than the night itself, swallowed him as the canopy above shut out the light of the moon. And then there was the silence. The creeping fear grew within him once more. He stepped on a twig. The snap sounded explosive and David froze, convinced that the witch had heard it. He stayed frozen for a long time, waiting for a sign that she was coming to get him. But there was only the dark and the silence and the pounding of his heart and the rushing of blood in his head.

Round and round he went, grabbing clumps of weeds. When he had as much as he could carry, he stood up straight and realised he didn't know where he was. He was lost. Fear gripped him again and he panicked. He ran and ran, bumping into the trees and tripping in the undergrowth, desperate to escape. Suddenly, the woods came to an end and he found himself beside the old mansion. The side windows were as jagged and ugly as the windows on the front of the house except that they were boarded up with rotting planks. From one of them the voice of the witch cut through the silence.

'Quickly! Quickly! Bring them out!'

David sprang back into the darkness as a sudden jolt of fear sliced through him. Then he heard the driver's cringing reply.

'I'm bringing them. I'm bringing them.'

What to do? As long as the witch was busy, he could examine his haul of plants. Clump by clump, his hands trembling, he held them up to the light of the moon but there wasn't any witchweed. It simply didn't grow in the woods. He would have to go out onto the open, moonlit ground where he could see huge swathes of it glinting just out of reach. Ten seconds was all it would take to dash out, grab a large handful and rush back under cover. But the witch was always alert. He could not know for certain that she hadn't sensed his presence already. If she even half suspected there was something wrong, she would be on the lookout and he couldn't stand up to the witch if she was prepared. Just a look from her could stop him. He had to make sure she suspected nothing.

He inched his way through the tall grass until he reached the mansion. He crept towards the boarded window and tried to peer inside. But the window was too far up for him. He tiptoed into the open and grabbed the nearest clump of witchweed and pulled. He was almost thrown forward by the resistance of the plant. He tugged and tugged but the plant clung to the ground as if held by wires of steel. He took out his penknife and with a trembling hand opened the blade. He sawed at the stem of the witchweed but his knife made no impression on it. It was hopeless. He gave the plant one last frantic tug, but it was no use. Everywhere he was surrounded by the very plant he needed to defeat the witch, but it was too tough to cut and so firmly rooted that he could not wrench it free.

From the corner of his eye he saw a sleek, black movement at the edge of the woods. He froze. And then he heard the meowing of a cat. Where was it? He scanned the edge of the trees where he'd sensed the movement but there was nothing to be seen. Slowly he moved towards the shadow of the mansion. Safe in darkness, his back against the wall of the house, his eyes darted this way and that, searching the grounds for any sign of the creature. He knew a cat was often a witch's familiar friend – an extension of her eyes, who could prowl around and warn her of danger. If the cat saw him, he was sunk. Still pressed hard against the wall, he inched his way towards the front of the house. As he reached the corner he saw the cat prowling in the distance and sniffing. He eased himself past the corner and peeked round. It was walking at a steady pace towards the mansion, towards him. He couldn't run across the open ground or the cat was sure to see him. He rushed to the gaping scar in the wall, scrambling over the rubble. The snarling blackness of it took his breath away and he fell back. But he had to hide, and the mansion was his only choice. As he climbed in, the blackness turned to grey and he saw that the entire room was filled with cobwebs as thick as cotton wool. In the gloom he saw the tiny forms of millions of little spiders and, as his hand brushed against the web, there was a rush of movement towards him. He staggered back in revulsion. He ran over the rubble and found himself by the two front doors. He knew the witch was busy elsewhere. Could he sneak in behind the doors and wait for the cat to go away? Another meow nearby told him he had no time to lose, as he clambered to hide behind the doors. He slipped inside and closed the door behind him.

What remained of the hallway was vast with a massive dilapidated old staircase that swept grandly upwards, dovetailing to the upper floor. It was intricately decorated with carvings and reliefs, but David could hardly see any of it. He was in a cavern – a tunnel in the vast web of spider's silk that surrounded him. This was where the regular comings and goings of the witch had made a way through the cobwebs. Here and there, on small tables, were skulls holding lighted black candles and topped by thin chimneys of charred and blackened web travelling towards the ceiling. But most gruesome of all were the skeletons of animals – mice, rats, squirrels and birds that hung with slackened, screaming jaws all through the web. They dangled there, hundreds of them, in postures of terror; the bones picked clean of flesh and only the mesh of the web keeping them intact.

The spiders had sensed David's presence and inched their way towards the edge of the web, towards him. Some were tiny and made their way speedily through the web. Others were as large as his hand. They were close to the ground and were much slower to react. They limbered up before delicately reaching out their hairy legs to feel their way along. But the truly terrifying ones were the medium-sized jet black spiders with red and yellow speckles. Their eyes were beady and their fangs two-pronged and sharp. Their long, sleek, graceful legs were like black knuckled needles and on their bodies they carried a shining, bloated, oozing bulb of poison. These moved without hurry, steadily picking their way through the web.

David felt the fear build inside him to a screaming panic. He turned back towards the door but already the smaller spiders were crawling all over it with the mid-sized poisoners not far behind. He pressed his arms tightly against his body and clamped his legs together. He shuffled backwards, away from the door; taking care in case any part of him, especially his hair, touched the cobweb. The spiders moved with him, crowding onto the edge of the web until it seemed to David the cavern was one writhing mass of creatures, waiting for this massive prey to fall victim to their million bites and poisonous fangs.

The floorboards creaked underfoot. He couldn't

carry on going backwards. He had no choice. He turned and scurried along as light-footed as he could across the uneven floor. He clasped one hand to his mouth to stop himself from screaming. The web vibrated around him as the spiders scuttled to catch up. He had to find some other exit. It was the stairs or nothing. The witch had made a vast passageway all the way up and David didn't even have to hold his arms in. Taking each step carefully, he climbed to the next floor. Here there were more skulls and black candles burning their charred chimneys into the fabric of the web and, in the gloomy light, he saw that this floor was a labyrinth of corridors and rooms, obscured by the ubiquitous web and the spiders that thronged around him, waiting for him to make one slip, one careless brush against their web. He wanted to find the window where he'd seen the witch. He thought he could climb through it and onto the portico. He didn't care anymore whether the cat saw him or not. He just wanted to escape. But in what direction? The sweeping curve of the staircase had made him lose his bearings again.

He hurried along the passage until he came to a large, panelled wooden door, the only one not obscured by cobwebs. He knew the witch was downstairs, so it might be safe to go through. He swallowed hard, turned the handle and found himself in a bedroom. It was like no other bedroom he'd ever seen. More skull-lanterns provided some light and a four-poster bed at the centre was free of the mesh of cobwebs that clung to the walls and ceiling. The bed was decorated, as was the rest of the room, with an intricate and corrupt blackness. The coverlet and pillows were embroidered with shining black thread. The bedside table was in dark wood covered in black mould. More mould clung to the walls behind the cobweb and to the furniture and the clothes draped around the room. Apart from the bed, the only other piece of furniture that dominated the room was the dressing table, with its huge oval mirror of burnished silver. It had tarnished to a dark, ugly brown. David caught sight of himself in it and stopped to stare. Wasn't it marvellous how handsome he was? That was always the way he imagined himself – although usually the mirror in the bathroom at home betrayed the truth. This mirror was far better. Much more to his liking. In this he could see just how firm and strong his features were. His build was athletic with a strong, muscular neck and broad shoulders. He was entranced. There was nothing to be afraid of. He could see that now. This brave, handsome, fine figure of a boy could sweep away all dangers. He was like a shining knight, not the frightened boy he'd imagined. He straightened his back and gazed proudly at his reflection in the mirror; his mind sinking ever deeper into the pleasure of delusion.

But from the corner of his eye he saw the legion of crawling spiders coming towards him. They were all frantic to be the first to get at him. He saw a large spider, making its way slowly and gracefully along the web as a hoard of smaller spiders raced along its body to get in front of it and beat it to the kill. Strong though the image in the mirror was, it was an illusion – and these spiders were real. David forced himself to remember his bathroom mirror and his true reflection. In the harsh morning light, with the glare of the bulb dazzling directly into his face, he wasn't all that handsome. He forced himself to remember the real him, not this beguiling fantasy. And the spiders were getting nearer. David knew that if he did nothing now then the last thing he would see in the mirror would be the spiders crawling all over him. And that would also be all too real.

David rushed to close the door – although he knew that wouldn't keep them back. And as he turned to find an escape route through the window he saw the witchweed. It was in a vase on a side table near the door. He wouldn't have to take all of it; just enough for the spell – and the witch might not even notice some of it was gone. But it was embedded in the mesh of cobweb and he would have to reach in to fetch it.

The smaller spiders were already through the gap at the bottom of the door and scurrying towards him. The spiders inside the bedroom had felt his presence and had been woken by the vibrations in the room. They were massing at the edge of the web; a million specks of eyes and spindly feelers pointing towards him and twitching. He had to do it now or run for the window empty-handed with no power against the witch. That would mean certain death. 'Do it now!' His brain was screaming at him. 'Do it now!' And as if sensing his thoughts, the spiders in the web crawled towards the witchweed.

One of them, larger than all the rest, was making its way directly between David and the plant. Its long thin fangs were deadly and it carried a huge, bloated sack of poison on its back. But strangely, David was struck by it's look of sadness. The eyes looked sick and weary of its world. It was the sadness of a creature who lived in hunger; its whole life nothing but a waiting, waiting and waiting for a victim. And all the while its sack of poison grew and became a heavier burden to carry. This spider was not fierce. All it wanted was to inject its poison and relieve itself of the weight it carried. And then to eat at last, with its little mouth full of sharp little teeth. But, sad or not, it was deadly.

David stepped forward, his teeth gritted against the fear and revulsion. He plunged his arm into the web and grabbed for the witchweed. The web itself seemed to suck him in, trying to embalm him in a living death. The spider arched its back and the sack of poison quivered. In a slow, graceful movement it reached out its longest legs towards David's arm. David grappled with the witchweed, trying to separate one sprig from the bunch. But they clung together. He'd planned to reach in for no more than a second before whipping his arm back out again, but the web bound them. He

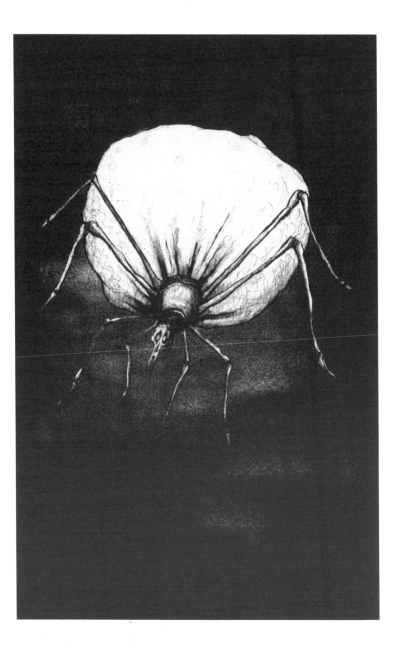

needed to use both hands to seperate them and he would have to be in the web far longer than he thought he could endure. Desperate for that one sprig, he plunged his other arm into the web. The little spiders were in a frenzy and almost at his feet. The poisoner could almost reach him with the tips of its long, thin legs. David grabbed hold of the clump of witchweed with one hand and yanked the free sprig out with the other. As soon as he had it free, he pulled his other arm out just as the poisoner brushed against his skin. The mass of web around the sprig of witchweed was crawling with tiny spiders. He beat them off on the floor and sent them scattering with the blows. Then he felt something dragging at his elbow. A mass of web was dangling from it, weighed down by the heavy body of the sad spider who was now creeping delicately up towards his arm, its mouth flapping open. David grabbed the web and flung it and the spider against the wooden door. Its sack exploded, splattering the other spiders with a poison that dissolved their bodies to a bubbling pulp.

The spider itself, freed from its burden, was scrabbling about. But without the sack it was off balance and its fangs stuck in the wooden floorboards. It struggled to get free, thrashing its legs about uselessly. The surviving smaller spiders took their revenge. They crawled all over it and ate it from the inside. David saw the last glimmer of sadness in its eyes before they were plucked inwards and consumed. In only a few seconds, it was nothing but a shell. Then the voice of Mrs GwraK came slicing through the room.

'What do you think you're doing?'

Her voice came from behind him and instantly the spiders fled under the door or back into the web. He had the witchweed in his hand but he couldn't remember a word of the spell, not even the first word. If he could just remember that first word he might have a chance.

'Turn around!'

David had no choice but to do as he was told. He turned around but she wasn't there. Then her voice shouted again.

'Don't you dare spill another drop, do you hear me?' David breathed a huge sigh of relief. Her voice was coming up from the floor. She must be in the room below. David noticed a crack in the floorboards and a light shimmering through. He knelt and looked down. The room was an old ballroom, long since decayed and dilapidated. At its centre a log fire blazed beneath an enormous cauldron and smoke and steam filled the air. The cowardly driver, who behaved more like a servant, was bringing in barrels through some old French windows, but the witch was impatient and angry. The poor man was exhausted but his cringing fear kept him scurrying about. He opened one of the barrels, lifted it and climbed the ladder to the rim of the cauldron. He was lucky not to burn his legs. He tipped the barrel over and poured the contents in.

There was a great whoosh of steam and a deafening, roaring sizzle as guts, entrails, back ends and nostrils, eyeballs and hooves, whole rats, slugs bubbling with slime and live cockroaches all gushed out of the barrel. The stench was incredible. The servant hurried back down the ladder to fetch another barrel and David pulled his face away to escape the horrible smell.

Then another smell swept over him like a wave. The rotten stench from the barrels was almost totally smothered by that familiar sickly savoury sweetness he remembered from the school dinners, making him dizzy. He covered his nose and mouth with his hand and peered once more into the room. The air was like a thick syrup, and yet the rotten stench still pervaded his nostrils. It mixed with the sickly sweetness in a putrid, choking miasma and he had to fight against the dizziness it caused.

Three of the barrels were empty, with another ten waiting to be opened. The witch had taken a sack and climbed the ladder to the cauldron. From this she was ladling spoonfuls of a fine powder into the mixture. Great clouds of it puffed up into the air as she shoved the ladle into the sack. It mixed with the smoke and the steam, making the air more unbreathable than ever. The servant was going berserk, licking the air with his thick, coarse tongue and sucking in great gulps of air as if he was trying to eat it. The witch stirred the mixture with a large wooden spoon in the shape of a paddle and cackled:

'Fatty, crisp and sweet or salty,
Good to make the children fat and ready.'

The light of the fire flickered on her face, contorting its look of demented delight as the servant cringed and begged and whimpered at the foot of the ladder. The witch dipped the ladle into the disgusting mixture and handed it to him. He clutched at it frantically and slurped a huge mouthful. David could see it was hardly cooked and a live cockroach escaped down his chin and disappeared under his shirt. Steam rose from the mixture but it was almost raw, yet slimy enough to slip smoothly into his mouth and down his throat. A rat's tail hung down from the corner of his mouth. He sucked it up like a piece of spaghetti and licked the juices from his lips. A feeling of nausea robbed David of all his strength. If this was the truth about the food, he would never be able to swallow even a tiny spoonful of it ever again; not even to fool the witch. Monday was less than two days away. If he didn't destroy her by Monday, he was bound to be caught.

The servant was so delighted with his treat that he tripped over one of the barrels and sent a mass of squirming entrails splashing onto the floor. The witch turned on him with a snarl.

'*I warned you.*' The poor servant whimpered at the thought of the punishment to come. He didn't even dare to apologise in case his words irritated the witch even more.

'You like the sugar that much, do you?' she mocked. The servant whimpered again, averting his eyes in fear and shame.

'Why don't you try some pure fatty sugar? That might make you happy!'

She threw the sack of powder at him. It struck him on the chest and a cloud of sugar flew into his face. He didn't know what to think! He knew he'd done wrong and he knew the witch was angry. But pure sugar was a treat, not a punishment! David saw the look of confusion on his face. His mouth gulped at the powder even as his eyes betrayed the certainty that this was a trap. But the witch just stood at the top of the ladder, looking down at him. He was permitted to eat the sugar! He grabbed the sack and stuck his face into it, letting the sugar pour down his throat as it flowed into his mouth like a liquid. When the sack was empty he looked at her with eyes that were glazed and empty. The witch remained still, waiting for the inevitable to begin. The servant saw the look in her eyes and knew for certain this was a punishment after all. The pain started in the pit of his stomach and grew to fill his lungs. Suddenly, he started to grow, expanding so quickly his skin twanged with the strain. He tried to cry out but his tongue burst out of his mouth. His whole body ballooned and in a moment he was on his back, kicking furiously. He couldn't even scream, but his hands still grabbed in search of any trace of sugar in the air. With a pop, he expanded into the shape of a perfect ball. The witch

8

climbed down and rolled the ball of human flesh up the ladder towards the rim of the cauldron. David looked away and covered his ears. But it didn't stop him hearing the witch as she carried on mixing, and humming a happy song.

hope·at·last

David slept late on Sunday morning after the terror of the night before. His arms still didn't feel right after the sensation of the web on his skin and he was plagued by the urge to scratch them and pull at his fingers; to rip the clinging web from them and take away the itch it had left behind. Sometimes his whole body would convulse at the thought of those spiders. He imagined them crawling all over him and a spasm of fear and disgust would twist his body and make him slap himself as he tried to kill the imaginary spiders. But worst of all was the memory of the witch's voice. Her voice, her real voice, was like a rusty, jagged cleaver cutting into him and his hands balled again into tight fists at the memory of it. When he saw what the witch was about to do to her servant, panic had swept over him. He saw the gaping mess he'd left in the web and rushed to smooth it over in the hope that she wouldn't notice. The witchweed he'd left behind seemed to hang in the web rather than go back in the vase but there was nothing he could do about that. He just had to tidy up as much as he could. Luckily, the spiders had all scurried back to their webs at the sound of the witch in anger. David hurried back down the corridor, found the stairs and rushed out into the night. He didn't care by then whether the cat saw him or not. He just had to get out. The cat wasn't anywhere to be seen but David felt sure the witch would know that someone had been to her lair last night. She might even know it was him. That worry nagged at him constantly now, but he knew there was no turning back. He had to fight, and to fight, he had to be prepared.

After breakfast he put his sprig of witchweed and his copy of the spell in his pocket and went for a walk. He needed to be outside, to have fresh air in his lungs, to see the world about him in daylight and erase that memory of the dark night and the sickness that clung to him. He stopped. That was strange. For all the horror of the cat and the spiders and skeletons, of actually being in the witch's bedroom and seeing for himself the ugly putrefaction of the food and the delight the witch took in killing – what really stuck in his memory was the mirror. He could have stood in front of it for the rest of his life and he would have been so happy, so contented. It told him how fantastic he was, and handsome, too. It had been spellbinding, the way his reflection seemed to glow. How much time, he wondered, did the witch spend sitting before it? And what did she see in its reflection? What was her vanity? Was it a weakness, maybe some need to feel goodness, however distorted.

The day was fresh and bright as David repeated the spell over and over in his head. The spell was obviously some kind of poem and David remembered the witch and her little rhyme.

'Fatty, crisp and sweet or salty,
Good to make the children fat and ready.'

Ready? Ready for what? She was preparing something and she was almost ready. The children were almost ready. But again, ready for what? He didn't know but he knew he had to prepare. He had to get her tomorrow or it would be too late. He made his way to the park and into the trees to say the words out loud and hear them properly. He was just clearing his throat and preparing himself for a first attempt when he heard a twig snap behind him. Was it the witch? He listened hard but the silence behind him was complete. If it was the witch, he could kill her now. He wasn't well prepared but he just might be able to do it. He spun round and there was Mrs Jones. She still had the wild look he had seen when he had called at her house. In fact, she looked even wilder than before. There were bits of moss and twigs in her hair but she looked stronger somehow than she had yesterday.

'Thank you, David,' she said and gave him a hug. 'Thank you so much. You saved me.'

'You're better?' exclaimed David.

'I'm better now. Thanks to you. I knew she was a witch but I didn't think anyone would believe me.'

'That's how I felt.'

'I was afraid,' continued Mrs Jones. 'I knew that the witch was going to harm you all but there was nothing I could do. It drove me mad. But now I'm going to fight. I don't know how but I am going to fight! I've built myself a little shelter over there in the undergrowth so the witch won't know where I am. But tell no one that you've seen me. Promise me that! Promise!'

'I promise,' he said. 'But I've got a way to fight the witch.'

'Don't you dare go anywhere near her!' she commanded. 'Do you hear me?'

'But Mrs Jones!' he began but she cut him off.

'Go now. Go!' she ordered him. 'I don't want to attract attention.' She turned him back towards the park and gently but firmly pushed him on his way. 'You'll hear from me again, but tell no one that I'm here and keep away from Mrs GwraK.'

She disappeared into the trees. David stood there in a daze. He thought it would be useless to go after her. For his own protection she would shush him and forbid him before he could even open his mouth. He gave the undergrowth one last hopeful look before turning to go home. If only she'd listen to him. They could work together. He knew how to destroy the witch and it had to be tomorrow because Mrs Jones wouldn't stand a chance against the witch.

A police car was parked outside his house when David arrived back home. Had Mrs GwraK found out about David? Did she know he wasn't hypnotised and was planning to destroy her? He knew how the witch operated. She'd made people believe Mrs Jones had put horrible stuff in the food and she'd made Miss Lauren look like a bad teacher. Nobody would believe them now because everyone thought they were mad, bad or both. What did the witch have in mind for him? He was already known as a bit of a dreamer and nobody liked him anymore, not even Gareth, his best friend. Had the witch noticed something? Had she seen that a sprig of witchweed was missing or that someone had been to her room? Did she suspect him? Had she sent for the police to make him look like a criminal?

He walked into the kitchen, looking as innocent as he could. His dad was sitting at the kitchen table, scowling, and his mum was leaning against the sideboard with her arms crossed. Also sitting at the kitchen table was Bryant, the policeman, who had talked to him the day before.

'Ah, there you are,' he said flatly. 'I've been waiting for you.'

'I went for a walk.'

'You seem to like long walks all of a sudden,' growled his dad.

David looked down at his shoes. There was a long silence. Why didn't they just tell him what the witch had told them? A stab of anger shot through him. The witch had set them onto him and he couldn't defend himself. His anger grew and came close to bursting.

They'd already been told a pack of lies by the witch; they might as well hear his side of it. Just tell them what that nice old lady was really like! Throw it at them! Tell them the real truth! He was going to get her tomorrow anyway. What did it matter anymore what anybody thought? He was going to destroy the witch and that was that!

'She… she… she…' stuttered David, tears of anger glazing his eyes. He couldn't get a proper sentence out of his mouth but he tried again:

'She… she… she…'

His mum rushed towards him and his dad's scowl vanished from his face.

'David,' cried his mum. 'What has she done to you?'

'She's poisoning the food!'

'She can't be!' said his dad.

'She can!' shouted David. Why couldn't they just believe?

'Did she tell you this? Did she boast about it?'

'No! She didn't tell me!' David was frantic by now.

'We know she put those snails and worms and that snake into the food,' said his mum.

'You knew it was her?' he exclaimed. This was incredible. They knew about the witch. But weren't they going to do something about it?

'But David,' his mum continued, trying to reassure him. 'She can't poison the food. She isn't allowed near the school. Not since she did all those horrible things.'

David stared at her, open-mouthed. What was she talking about? Then his dad got up from his chair and hugged him.

'Is that what's bothering you?' he asked. 'Is that why you've been acting so strangely? You think Mrs Jones is somehow able to get at the food and poison it. Is that why you went to see her yesterday?'

So that was it! David thought they were talking about his night-time raid on the witch, and all the time they were talking about his visit to Mrs Jones! What had he said? He'd accused the witch of poisoning the food and they thought he was accusing Mrs Jones.

'No! No! It wasn't her!' he shouted.

'There, there, David,' his mum consoled him. 'She can't harm you now.'

Bryant got to his feet.

'David? A neighbour reported to us that Mrs Jones was visited yesterday by a boy. The description of that boy fits you exactly. Was it you?'

David nodded his head. How could he deny it?

'The neighbour reported some shouting and the boy left very upset. Is this true?'

David nodded again and Bryant put away his notebook. He bent down to be face to face with him and added:

'You wanted to know the truth, didn't you, David?'

'Yes.'

'And you found out the truth didn't you?'

David could have answered yes. He had found out the truth but Bryant meant something different. He meant that Mrs Jones was bad but David knew she was good. And so David said nothing. It was too late now. They thought they knew it all and so they just weren't going to listen.

'Shortly afterwards, Mrs Jones left her home carrying a bag and hasn't been seen since. She has disappeared off the face of the earth.'

He looked pointedly at David.

'Do you know where she is?'

David hesitated for a split second. He couldn't help it. He wasn't a very good liar and this was a policeman. He'd been trained to detect lies. But Mrs Jones had made David promise not to tell anyone where she was. He had to keep that promise.

'No,' he said. 'I don't know where she is.'

There was a pause and then Bryant said: 'There is one thing you must know. Mrs Jones is a criminal.'

'A criminal?' David was shocked.

'Yes, and now she's on the run,' replied Bryant. 'She put toxic material into children's food. If you see her, or know anything about her, you must tell me.'

David nodded his head.

'Okay,' said Bryant. 'I'll be on my way.'

He ruffled David's hair and set off.

'I only wanted to see that she was alright,' said David. 'I just want everything to be alright. I didn't like Mrs Jones to be hurt.'

'It's alright, David,' his mum said once Bryant had left. 'We didn't realise how upset you were at losing Mrs Jones and then Miss Lauren.'

'But you've got to leave things to the police,' added his dad. 'Tomorrow is my first day at my new job. The factory's going to open soon and there's a lot to prepare. Don't hang on to these strange ideas. When the police catch Mrs Jones, they'll take care of her.'

'They'll do everything for the best,' his mum said.

So, the witch was going to win if he didn't do something. He felt sure that if only Bryant could meet Mrs GwraK, he would see that she was a witch. It was only a small chance but at least it was better than nothing.

'I forgot to say something to the policeman,' said David and rushed out. He hoped he wasn't too late but when he got outside, Bryant was calmly leaning against the bonnet of his car, waiting for him.

'Was there something you couldn't tell me in front of your parents?' he asked.

David nodded and Bryant continued: 'Tell me. Tell me now where I can find Mrs Jones.'

'She didn't put that stuff in the food,' David protested.

'Yes,' replied Bryant. 'I can see you believe that. Your parents didn't notice the way you changed your story in there. But I did. You said "she's poisoning the food" and then you said "no she didn't". You believe someone's poisoning the food.'

At last, here was somebody who might listen and put a stop to Mrs GwraK. Maybe he could destroy the witch with the spell. He was a policeman and a grown-up and he was braver than David.

'Who do you think is poisoning the food?' asked Bryant.

'If you come to the school at lunchtime, you might see for yourself.'

Bryant considered this for a moment and David added: 'But don't show your feelings to anyone. If you see what I want you to see, pretend to be happy. It's the only way.'

'Alright,' replied Bryant. 'You're obviously upset and I have to admit that there is something strange going on at that school. But first things first. Where is Mrs Jones?'

'I can't tell you! She made me promise!'

Bryant stood up.

'Look, David. This is a proper police matter, not some fight in a school playground. You must tell me what you know. I'll come to the school tomorrow if you tell me where she is.'

'When you come to the school tomorrow,' David offered, 'I'll tell you where she's hiding.'

Bryant gaped at him. 'Are you trying to offer me some kind of deal?'

'Yes.'

'You don't offer me a deal like that. You tell me where she is right now!'

But David stood his ground. He couldn't break his promise and after a while Bryant relented.

'I suppose I'll have to accept your deal,' Bryant said. 'But I'm telling you this. Today, I'm going to look for Mrs Jones and if I find her, I won't be at that school tomorrow. But I will be back here and you will be in more trouble than you could ever imagine for withholding information from the police and allowing a criminal to go free.'

alone against the Witch

Monday morning dragged on and on but there was no sign of Bryant. David was the only normal kid in the school. He was his own natural shape and because of this he stood out. The witch was sharp and would know at a glance that he hadn't eaten her food. He'd be lucky to survive to the end of the day looking like this and there was nothing he could do to disguise himself. Bryant had to turn up at lunchtime because the witch would know for certain that David was her enemy. She could frighten him to such a nervous state that he would stammer and be unable to recite the spell. She could attack him before he had a chance to take the witchweed out of his bag. She had all the weapons of being fearsome and sly and cunning and watchful and very, very powerful. He had only a little bravery. True, he had the means to destroy her but it depended finally on his guts, and he didn't feel very gutsy.

And so the morning dragged on. The new teacher hadn't found his feet in the job and didn't know the names of the children. But he tried to be enthusiastic even though he'd had his share of the Golden Food. His energy lasted about half an hour before the relentless apathy of the class and his own lethargy overwhelmed him. He gave up and just handed out sums. The children just stared at them, not even lifting a pencil. David looked at the sums. He knew he could do them but he had too much to think about. Only a few days ago this had been a thriving school and he'd had nothing on his mind. He had no worries except being caught daydreaming. Then he remembered. Keep it normal. He had to keep it normal and avoid any trouble. David sat up straight in his seat and, difficult as it was to keep his mind off the witch, he did the sums. He was the only one scribbling away and quite soon he'd done them all. He took the sheet over to the teacher who looked at him in amazement.

'Have you actually done them?' he asked, waking out of a slumber.

'Yes, sir,' David replied.

'Is this some kind of joke? Are you playing some kind of game?' the teacher demanded.

'No, sir!' protested David. 'I've done the sums.'

The teacher huffed his annoyance at him and took the sums. Without even looking at them, he laboriously marked the sheet with one big tick. He handed them back to David and had another nap.

David didn't have anything to do now. He thought about the witch but that was too painful. This close to the confrontation, his mind resisted even the idea of her, in case it would drive him mad. He wanted something to occupy his mind but there was nothing and the minutes dragged slowly on. He'd do anything to have a little schoolwork to do – anything to occupy his mind. Looking out of the window just wasn't interesting anymore and he had to endure the tense boredom of waiting as the minutes hardly ticked by at all. At breaktime all the children listlessly shuffled out of the class and onto the yard. There, they just hung about. But the schoolyard was a dangerous place for David. He had to hide in case the witch saw him. Even the teachers had rolls of fat bulging out of their necks and flopping over their collars. Mr Williams had completely lost touch with reality and went about the yard greeting various children as if there was nothing wrong. Then they all shuffled back to the classes and the torture of time dragging on started all over again. Where was Bryant?

Finally, the lunch bell rang and a buzz of excitement energised the children. The classroom, twice as crowded as usual because of the growing bulk of the overfed children, was stifling and the sweat of excitement filled it and made it airless. Bryant simply hadn't arrived. Had he caught Mrs Jones? That was possible but he just had to get here during lunch!

There was a huge jam of children in the doorway as they jostled to be first to the canteen. The new teacher had no hope of controlling them.

'No rushing there, children!' he shouted. It was obvious from the look on his face and the way he tried to force himself through the crowd that he was as desperate as everyone else to get at the food. He tried using his teacher's authority to make a path through the crowded bodies, but they ignored him.

Slowly, and with a lot of squeezing, one by one the

children got through the door. David sneaked into the middle of them, hoping to use them as cover. He was pushed and jostled and squashed in the throng as he made his way to the canteen.

Adrian hadn't forgotten him, of course. He came puffing towards him and laid a dough-like hand on his shoulder. What would happen to Adrian if he ate another portion? He was already much, much fatter than any of the other kids. He was even fatter than Gareth who had also followed him to the table. There wasn't a lot of room for David but at least he was well hidden.

Table by table, they queued for the Golden Food. This was going to be tricky. If the witch was helping to serve she'd know he hadn't eaten any of her revolting junk even though she'd given him a double portion on Friday. She would see two extra large children beside him and she would easily guess the truth, that the doctor's hypnotic spell had been broken. But he had to join the queue as it moved forward inch by inch. The noise was disgusting. Gone were the lolling heads, the air-licking and the constant 'ungungung-ing'. Instead, there was an insistent, high-pitched whining moan that got louder and louder as the food was served. David tried to join in, but it was difficult. He croaked a half-hearted version of it that just didn't sound right. He didn't look the part and he didn't sound the part of a child who'd gorged himself on the Golden Food, and she was bound to notice him as he got closer and closer to the hatch. With incredible luck, when his turn came she was busy at the sink with the massive pots and pans that were too big for the dishwasher.

One of the kitchen assistants listlessly plopped a greasy, fried pat of Golden Food onto his plate and the thick fat oozed out of it. He hurried back to his table before the witch saw him and kept an eye on the canteen doors, expecting Bryant to appear at any moment. He was late. Had he made some mistake? Didn't he know when lunch was served at the school? Had he caught Mrs Jones and was busy questioning her? Maybe he didn't care after all. But that wasn't like him. He would have shown up anyway to find out what was going on in the school. Perhaps he was delayed by something. A lot of things could delay adults that David didn't understand. Perhaps it was something like that. It must be, because he hadn't turned up and David was faced with this plateful of gunk. The thought of eating it turned his stomach and made his belly crawl and twist in a knot. He remembered, more starkly than before, the mixture of entrails, rats and insects that went into the food. And he remembered the servant being rolled up the ladder towards the cauldron. He'd smelt the putrefaction, smothered by the artificial perfume of savoury sweetness.

Gareth had finished his portion almost at a single swallow and globs of golden grease dripped down his chins. He looked directly at David with remorse.

'I'm sorry for saying I didn't like you,' he said thickly.

David's heart leapt. Gareth wanted to be his friend again. There was hope! Even if he was alone against the witch, she wasn't powerful enough to destroy friendship. And then he saw Gareth's eyes flicker down towards his pat of uneaten food. It was only a small flicker but it was enough. Gareth was sucking up to him in the hope of getting his food. His best friend was being false and scrounging. David remembered the time when Gareth had been so excited about his new bike. It was rugged, with a suspension system for rough terrain. It was much better than David's bike and they both knew it. It was like their ultimate vision of what a bike should be. Gareth was so excited he'd cycled all the way to David's house to show it. But he wasn't boasting or showing off. He was just so excited and had to share his excitement with his best friend. He offered him a go on his bike straight away. That was Gareth: open, kind and sharing. The best friend you could ever have.

But the witch had changed him and a wild anger towards Mrs GwraK boiled up in David. He knew he had to control that anger and not let it flare up. He had to take strength from it but not go off the rails. But he was in a tight spot. Adrian was expecting a full extra portion, but David had seen what too much Golden Food could do. Adrian's face and body were already so enlarged that his eyes were just two small glinting slits buried deep in his head and his skin was stretched almost to bursting. The last thing David wanted was for Adrian to actually explode next to him in the canteen. Gareth was looking at David, unaware his false apology had been found out. He was still hoping to get an extra share of food but David didn't want to give him any. Gareth and Adrian were already much larger than the other children. It wouldn't be right to give them any more, but they'd get nasty if he gave it to someone else. If only Bryant would show up. That hope nagged at him. Maybe the witch had got wind of his plan. No. Bryant had found Mrs Jones and he wasn't coming. Now David had to get through lunch without arousing suspicion and then attack the witch alone.

David kicked Adrian's leg under the table. He took this as a signal and shoved his plate out but all he got was a warning look and a small shake of David's head. David quickly flicked his eyes towards Gareth. Adrian understood. He was being warned that Gareth would get angry if he got the food. Then David turned to Gareth and silently mouthed the word 'later' to him. Gareth understood. David couldn't give him the food in front of Adrian. David snatched the food from his plate and shoved it up his jumper. He winked at Adrian.

It had worked. Both Adrian and Gareth now believed they would get an extra share later on and they were happy. Just at that moment Mrs GwraK arrived at the table. She stood directly in front of David and he sensed that she knew he hadn't eaten his portion of Golden Food. Did she also know about the witchweed and the spell? Fear shot through him. Then his anger quelled the fear and he held her stare. There was plain, blank contempt in his defiance. He was playing a dangerous game, but he was tired of the deceit, tired of cringing. Let her think he was just a little boy. Even if she knew about his secret weapon, she would be too arrogant to be afraid and that would lead to her destruction.

The witch looked surprised, but this was a public place and David knew she'd try to have her revenge in some sneaky way. After lunch, while all the other children were moping about in a stupor, he would find the witch. She would toy with him like a cat with a mouse, enjoying her little game. And then he would produce the witchweed and the tables would be turned.

The witch paused and a grey flame flickered deep within her eyes. David felt the force of her magnetism but he resisted it. He felt her attempt to peer into his mind and felt again that floating feeling growing within him. But by sheer willpower he held on to himself and the feeling faded away. There was another flicker of surprise from the witch as she contemplated what to do next, and then she withdrew. David saw the look in her eyes and he was ecstatic. At last he'd defied Mrs GwraK and he couldn't wait to confront her and turn her into dust.

Finally, the children were released into the playground. It was easy for David to escape from

Gareth and Adrian by just walking away. They huffed and puffed as they came after him, reaching out and trying to grab him for the food he'd promised. Even the effort of walking was too much for them and they fell back, out of breath. The last he saw of them, they were arguing and squabbling – blaming each other for not getting that extra portion. They started hitting each other with useless slow blows that bounced off the flesh. It only lasted a short while before they collapsed breathlessly on the ground.

David marched straight towards the back door of the kitchen and waited for Mrs GwraK to come out. She would be confident and sneering. He would laugh at her and take the witchweed out of his bag.

David muttered the spell over and over to himself. And then the witch came striding out of the kitchen. She towered over him, threatening and ready to strike. She gave him a mocking look, as if to ask what feeble effort David would make to destroy her.

'What do you think you're going to do, little boy?'

David knew what he had to do but his urge to attack her was too strong. Instead of reaching for the witchweed, he pulled the pat of food from under his jumper and threw it at her. It splattered on her face, making a greasy stain.

'Keep your filthy food, you witch!' he shouted. 'You won't get me to eat it!'

'I don't need you to eat it,' she taunted. 'I have other ways and means at my disposal.'

'Oh, yeah?' countered David. 'Like your servant? The one you killed!' The witch gave a look of surprise and David got a grip on his anger. He reached into his bag and took out the witchweed. He held it in front of her, his hand shaking. He could see the fear in her eyes. He had the upper hand but the witch was recovering and gathering her strength. The furious grey flame flickered in her eyes but David brandished the witchweed again. The flame withered but it didn't die. It would take the spell to do that. His throat was dry and his lips felt stiff. There wasn't any spit in his mouth. The witch held him in her stare and tried to scowl but her fear showed through and robbed her of the power to make him afraid. Stuttering at first, but then with confidence; David uttered the spell:

Yn·drech·na·grym·ac·hud·y·Wrach — a·thrwy
hyn·ei·throi'n·gawlach,
yn·llwch·dyma·swyn·holl·iach
fel·saeth·i·falu·sothach.

The witch's stare grew wild. Her mouth dropped open. Finally there was a pleading look before the fire in her eyes died.

David could breathe at last. He took in great gulps of air as the shock of success overtook him. The wave of relief at finally defeating the witch almost

made him collapse as he felt all his fear flow out of him like a liquid being drained. He felt exhausted and thought he could sleep forever but there was one more thing left to do. The witch stood before him, frozen by the spell. He stepped slowly toward her. It was like approaching some prickly, poisonous creature tranquillised by a dart. He knew it was safe to approach but it was still fearsome. Inch by inch he approached her; his heart thumping in the quiet that surrounded him. When he got close enough he reached out and touched her with the witchweed. The reaction was instant. The witch flicked her head towards him, the grey flame flaring up more furious than ever before.

'Ah-ha!' she cackled. 'You've fallen into my trap! Now I have you in my grasp!'

David staggered back. Fear sliced through him; a storm of panic sweeping across his brain, jumbling his thoughts into a dizzy mess. The witch was alive! The fear that had drained out of him returned, striking him like a tidal wave. He felt himself drowning in his own terror as his breath was stolen from him.

'Do you know how to destroy a witch?' she gloated. 'Do you know? Tell me! Tell me how!'

Her face was made even more hideous by her ecstatic glee. Only a short while ago David had been ecstatic. That had been part of the trap – to give him victory and a release from the nightmare, before plunging him back into the jaws of a terror many times worse.

'You are a very special boy,' she continued. 'Not like all these other children. You found my website. That told you how to slay me. But of course it was all a pack of lies!'

She snatched the witchweed from him.

'A beautiful little plant isn't it? I grow it wherever I go. It is, of course, poisonous.'

So that was it. Whoever wanted to kill her would find her false website and follow the instructions. The spell and the herb were harmless to the witch but it would bring her enemies out into the open.

'You've been brave enough to defy me,' she gloated. 'You've been loyal to your friends and you have imagination. When I take those qualities and twist them to my purpose – I will sculpt you into my perfect servant.'

'No!' he shouted. 'Never!'

'Oh yes, David. I've had an eye on you from the start. You could see through my disguise. I knew that from the first time I saw you. You have spirit. I will crush and drain that spirit, and then you'll do my bidding. That will be your fate, to be my servant in all things. Firstly I'll have to hypnotise you. But a mesmerised servant is a very poor thing, far too mechanical. As time goes on, you will grow to love your work and love to serve me.'

David turned and ran. He ran with the force of panic, bumping into the children in the playground. And all the while he could hear the cackle of the witch in his ears:

'Run, David! Run! I'll catch you! Hide away, hide! I'll find you and when I've drained you of all feeling, then you will be mine!'

David slammed into the school gates and fumbled with the catch. He felt the witch was about to grab him even though he knew she was letting him run. She could catch him anytime, no matter what he did. He was running out of school at lunchtime and the witch could use that against him. He was breaking the rules and that could be used to snare him, to make him look bad and turn everyone against him. He was trapped. Even running away was falling into her trap.

He ran towards the park in the hope of seeing Mrs Jones. She would understand. But if he ran to her, the witch would find her. And what could Mrs Jones do in any case? She was an old woman and the witch had dealt with her once already. He couldn't put her in danger.

Bryant was his last hope now. He had to get to him. He hadn't turned up at the school but he couldn't ignore a cry for help. He'd tell him the truth this time. The witch was letting him escape in order to catch him again. That was her idea of fun: to soften him up and prepare him to be her servant. But he had this one last hope.

David kept on running until, out of breath, he arrived home. He found the spare key but, because his hand was shaking so much, he struggled to put it in the lock. Eventually he managed it, opened the door and almost fell into the house. He shut the door and felt safe at last. He was home, locked behind his own front door. Then fear gripped him again. The house was silent. Was it really too silent? What if the witch was already here? Was she waiting for him? Waiting for the moment when he felt safe at last before pouncing? If the witch was waiting for him to feel safe, then feeling safe was the most dangerous thing of all.

'Come on, then!' shouted David. He was exhausted. If the witch wanted him, just let her come and get him. But there was only the silence. The phone was around the corner of the hallway. He had to get to it. He fumbled for the card with Bryant's phone number and steadied himself. He pressed himself against the wall and slowly peered round the corner. There was nobody there. He tiptoed towards the phone and gently lifted the handset. The click sounded so loud. He read the numbers on the card and punched them out on the keypad. It rang and rang and rang and David felt sure the witch had got to Bryant. Then he heard his voice:

'This is the voicemail of Police Constable Bryant. I'm sorry but I'm not at my desk at the moment. Please leave a message with your name and number after the tone and I'll try to get back to you.'

It was his answering service! What could he do now? He couldn't leave a message about the witch! That would sound crazy. What could he say? Then the tone 'beeped' and David cried out:

'Help me! Help me, please! I'm in trouble and I need your help! Please! Please! Before it's too late! I'm at home and I've run away from school! Please help me, please!'

He slammed the phone down, hoping against hope that Bryant would get his message soon and be on his way. David didn't know what even a policeman could do against the witch but at least he could call on other policemen for help. He could cause enough trouble to make things difficult for Mrs GwraK. A lot of people would start asking questions. And the witch wouldn't like that. She liked to keep things quiet. But it all depended on one thing; Bryant had to be able to see she was a witch. Please let him be like Miss Lauren – an adult who could see through the disguise. If he couldn't see the truth, the witch might have time to twist things around and make David sound like a liar. That mustn't happen! Bryant was the only hope he had left! He had to see the truth or David would be forced into slavery as the servant of a witch, obeying her orders and helping her destroy other children for all eternity. The thought of it burned his brain and he fainted, falling heavily on the floor of the hallway.

He felt time passing. He hadn't eaten since breakfast and his hunger gnawed at him. He felt tired and weak. Was this the witch's doing? Had she cast a spell on him?

He could hear his parents calling him from a distance. He opened his eyes and their voices were instantly closer. His mum was peering at him, a look of terrible worry on her face. His mum and dad! Someone had called his parents! He was going to be alright!

'Oh, David,' she cried as she hugged him. 'We've been so worried.'

'It was frightening,' said his dad, his face looming over him. He was eating a biscuit. It made David think he hadn't been all that frightened after all.

'Sorry, dad,' he said, remembering it had been the first day at his new job. 'I couldn't keep it normal.'

'That's okay,' replied his dad cheerfully, and still chewing on that biscuit. 'They were alright about me leaving early. It was an emergency and they couldn't do enough to help me.'

David was glad about that. He didn't like to let his parents down.

'And I'll tell you who's been really helpful,' said his mum. 'Your favourite dinner lady.'

Favourite dinner lady? Mrs Jones? How could that be? He looked past his mother and sat bolt upright. Standing tall and dark in his kitchen was the witch. She was smiling kindly at him but it was a mockery of kindness. She was mocking him, gloating at her victory.

'Hello, David. I'm so glad to see you're alright.'

'She's the one who phoned,' continued his mum.

His favourite dinner lady?!

'She's come over to see you're alright and she's

'helped us make you comfortable,' added his mum with a note of innocent gratitude in her voice.

'I was so concerned for you,' said the witch. 'I thought you'd had some sort of fit.'

David stared at her, at a loss for words. Then he sprang up and rushed past his parents.

'You made me have that fit!' he accused her. 'You're the one who's done this and now you're pretending to be nice. You're not my favourite dinner lady! That's Mrs Jones! The one you got rid of!'

The witch gave a look of wounded surprise.

'Don't believe a word she tells you!' pleaded David to his parents, but when he turned round they were both fast asleep. His dad was slumped back in his chair with half a biscuit in his hand. His mouth gaped open, showing a mouthful of chewed up pulp. His mum sat on one of the other chairs, her head slumped forward. David saw a few crumbs at the corner of her mouth.

'I do make a very nice biscuit,' mocked the witch.

'Is that the same stuff as the food?' he shouted at the witch as fury coursed through his veins. 'Did you make my mum and dad eat that filth?'

The witch laughed with her real witch's cackle that stabbed at him like sharp little knives.

'You witch!' he roared and now he really did attack her. He beat at her with his fists but she just laughed. It was a last hopeless effort and the witch mocked him for it. They both knew this was the end for him.

He'd lost the battle and he would be forced to become one of her servants. She was just too powerful. He had to strike her. There was nothing else he could do, but every blow he struck was useless and drained his energy. Perhaps that's what the witch wanted – she was waiting until he was completely drained of his energy and willpower. Once empty, the witch could fill him with her thoughts and make him think the same as her. He felt himself tiring. He couldn't cry any longer, there were no tears left. And the more he fought, the more he fell into her clutches.

He staggered back, exhausted from throwing so many punches. He hadn't hurt the witch at all. But then he saw Bryant standing in the kitchen doorway. He'd arrived! Almost too late, but he had arrived!

'Look at her!' shouted David, pointing. 'She's a witch! Please tell me you can see it! Look what she's done to mum and dad! Can't you see she's a witch?'

'I can see she's a witch,' he said as he held out his hand to him. 'Circle round her and come towards me. Think of her like a cobra and circle round slowly.'

The witch stood where she was, the look of surprise gradually fading from her face. Her eyes narrowed, as she calculated what to do next. David crept away from his sleeping parents and round towards Bryant. The witch followed him with her eyes. Round David went and when he got close to Bryant he rushed towards him and clasped his hand. Bryant pulled David behind him, putting himself between David and the witch.

The witch turned her gaze towards Bryant but he held it.

'I don't know what to do next,' said Bryant nervously. 'That Mrs Jones, she's a wise old woman, isn't she?'

'Yes.'

'She might know what to do,' he continued. 'Or, if this witch wants to get at her, she'll need protection. Tell me. Where is she?'

'I can't tell you! She'll hear me say it.' He pointed at the witch who seemed to have recovered her confidence and was grinning at them.

'Whisper it quietly to me. I can radio a team to collect her and bring her here,' said Bryant and he bent down.

David cupped his hands over his ear and whispered: 'She's hiding in the woods by the park.'

Bryant nodded and stood up straight. He faced the witch and said: 'Mrs Jones is hiding in the woods by the park. Shall I go and get her or do you want to deal with her yourself?'

David reeled away in shock but Bryant gripped his wrist and pulled him back. For a moment, he thought he'd misheard. Bryant had told the witch where to find Mrs Jones! Then he understood. Bryant was a servant of the witch.

'Find that woman and bring her to me,' ordered the witch. 'I have work to do here.'

Bryant left the kitchen without a single word to

David. The witch approached him and he felt the last of his energy drain away. The witch held him in her gaze and he was overcome by a heavy wave of sleep. He was powerless to resist.

the future belongs to me

David woke up feeling groggy. For a while his thoughts were jumbled and he couldn't see straight. Then with a sinking heart he remembered it all – the failure of the magic spell, his parents fast asleep, Bryant's betrayal and the witch looming over him, cackling. He blinked his eyes to clear them and shook his head. He tried to move but he couldn't. He was securely tied with thick ropes. He struggled and pulled but it was no use. He was in some sort of factory, high up on a large metal platform. All about him was gloomy but he could just about make out a weird labyrinth of wrought iron staircases, some of them spiral leading to other platforms. It reminded him of the mansion with its gate and staircase. It was all so ornate and old-fashioned. The metal was tarnished and already the spiders were claiming their places. And yet he sensed it was all new. The spiders had only just started to colonise the various nooks and crannies made by the tangled shapes of the metal. Their cobwebs had yet to grow to fill the space as they had done in the mansion. On either side were staircases leading down to an even greater gloom. A faint smell of that sickly sweet powder drifted towards him from above. As he gradually came to his senses he realised he was tied up next to Mrs Jones.

'I'm sorry,' he told her. 'They tricked me. I thought

Bryant was a friend but he was a servant of the witch.'

'It's alright,' she reassured him. 'This witch is full of tricks.'

'But it's my fault you're here.' David was more upset at betraying her than he was about his own capture. But Mrs Jones refused to blame him.

'The only one to blame is the witch,' she said.

As she spoke, the witch climbed the stairs, out of the darkness and onto the platform. She stood before them, her face a picture of gloating hatred.

'Now my child,' she said to David, 'your training can begin.'

She clicked her fingers and David's dad came up the stairs and stood beside her. So this was the factory where he had started work! Was he a part of her plan? Had he secretly become one of her servants? It couldn't be! Not dad!

The witch clicked her fingers again and his dad stood up straight, ready for action. The witch beckoned him forward and pointed to Mrs Jones.

'What would you do with her?' she asked gleefully.

'Kill,' he answered. 'Slay the enemies of Mrs GwraK.'

David couldn't believe it. What had that witch done to his father! Then she pointed at David.

'And him?' she asked slyly. 'What would you do to him?'

'Kill,' he answered. 'Slay the enemies of Mrs GwraK.'

'But he's your son,' she protested with false concern.

'Slay the enemies of Mrs GwraK,' he repeated.

The witch was delighted with her demonstration but Mrs Jones soon wiped the smile from her face.

'Now you're over-egging the pudding,' she goaded her. 'It's obvious he's been hypnotised. He wouldn't really want to kill his son.'

That was why the witch hated Mrs Jones so much. She had age and experience and could get under her skin. True, the witch had made her insane for a time but Mrs Jones had soon recovered and was ready for revenge, if she could only get herself free of the ropes.

'For that insult,' hissed Mrs GwraK, 'I will let you live to witness the horror I have prepared.'

She clicked her fingers at David's father and commanded him: 'Go and prepare for our night of slaughter. To your station and be ready to throw the switch.'

He turned and went back towards the stairs.

'Dad!' David called out as the shadows engulfed him. 'Dad, please! It's me, David! Please don't! Dad! Dad! She's a witch! Dad! Dad!'

For a moment, his father stopped and turned to look at David.

'Dad!' David pleaded. 'Dad! Dad!'

With a gesture from the witch, he turned away and went down the stairs. The witch turned towards her prisoners.

'You have a wonderful view,' she said like a gracious host. She snapped her fingers and here and there strange lights began to glow. They deepened the gloom about them but they highlighted the specific devices within the factory. The massive tangle of staircases and platforms became clearer and David saw the wisps of cobwebs shimmer as the spiders went scuttling about, hard at work. Above them was an enormous metal canister, reeking of that vile sugar. A smooth pipe of thin metal ran down from it, through a hole in the platform and down to a vast cauldron made of thick metal with a huge mixing paddle jutting down from a large motor. But the real horror was the sight of the grinder below. Large wheels covered in blades were set against other, smaller wheels, also covered in blades. Together they formed the face of an angry demon with a dark mouth where the blades interlaced. A thousand points of brightness glistened on its face where the sharp edges of the blades reflected the strange light. But in the crevices between the blades, scum had already formed as if instant decay pervaded every creation of the witch.

'The wheels spin very fast and the teeth are very sharp,' the witch boasted. Then she left them to supervise the arrangements. As she reached the stairs she paused to say to David: 'Your father is in charge of the switch that turns these grinders on. You will know that he has committed the slaughter that is about to take place. And when you realise that, I will come for you and make you mine.'

Now, no aspect of the horror was hidden. The witch was showing off her power and gloating at what she was about to do. She cackled at the thought of it and went down the metal stairs.

As soon as she was out of sight Miss Lauren popped her head up from where she'd been hiding. She had climbed the network of metal struts that held up the platforms, careful to keep in the shadows but when the lights had suddenly come on, she'd rushed to reach the top platform before she was seen.

'Shshshsh. Don't say anything. It's me,' whispered Miss Lauren.

They turned round in surprise and frantically urged her to let them go.

'Untie the ropes,' said Mrs Jones.

'Get us out of here,' said David.

'I said shshshsh!' whispered Miss Lauren. 'I can't right now. She might come back.'

'Get us out of these ropes!' they both protested but Miss Lauren shushed them again.

'I know how to kill her,' she announced. 'But I need to take her by surprise or I might lose my nerve.' She brandished a large sprig of witchweed. 'I went to a lot of trouble to get this,' she said, suddenly scratching her hair and wiping her face with her hand, but before

David could warn her she shot off after the witch.

'What's the matter, David?' asked Mrs Jones, surprised at his worried expression.

'It's a trap. There's a website that gives you a spell to kill her. But the witch set it up.'

'That plant is actually harmless?'

'Yes. I fell into the trap and now Miss Lauren is going to do the same.'

Mrs Jones thought a moment. 'Okay, but we still have some hope. What was the spell?'

'You collect a herb called witchweed. It's supposedly deadly to the witch. You hold it in front of her and chant a kind of poem. That freezes the witch, or it was supposed to. And then you touch her with the witchweed and she's supposed to turn to dust.'

'Hmm. That does sound a bit too easy, a bit too ready-made.'

'I thought it sounded convincing.'

'When something's just a little too easy, you should be suspicious.'

'I suppose so.'

'Well, if I know that witch, Miss Lauren will be safe for now. You can bet she'll tie her up with us here first. Look at these lights showing us everything. We're like an audience for her. She's the sort who'll make a meal of showing off to her enemies.'

Just as Mrs Jones had foreseen, a very sad Miss Lauren was led back up the stairs by the doctor who had hypnotised David.

'I'll just tie you up here until it's time for you to be dealt with,' he said in his usual jolly voice. 'I do hope you're comfortable.'

David was despondent. If the witch succeeded in her plans then neither Mrs Jones nor Miss Lauren would be alive to see the morning and David would become a disgusting wretch. What would she make him do? Kill Mrs Jones and then Miss Lauren? Would that be his first task?

After tying Miss Lauren next to David and Mrs Jones, the doctor went back to his work in charge of the industrial mixing mechanism.

The three of them sat in despair as the witch returned and paraded in front of them.

'This is a surprise,' she gloated to Miss Lauren. 'I didn't think I'd have to bother with you again. But I am glad to see you. I had marked you down for death and this is far more convenient for me, all my enemies together and in my grasp.'

She cackled insanely but Mrs Jones cut her off: 'Why do you bother with all this show? Why don't you just get on with it?'

'I will, I will,' replied the witch gleefully. 'But don't be so boring. I could do so much with just a snap of my fingers – but where's the fun in that?'

Mrs Jones crinkled her nose in disgust as the witch ran her hand along the large tube leading down from the canister.

'You won't succeed,' said Miss Lauren. The witch

ignored her and strode to the railings of the balcony and called down:

'Open the main door and let the grinding begin!'

Bryant pressed a switch and an electric motor began to raise the huge shuttered factory door. Outside stood all the children from school, dazed and almost oblivious as to what was happening. And leading them into the factory was Mr Williams. He seemed to be under the illusion that this was a school trip to see the new factory. He was very enthusiastic.

'Forward, children. Come along,' he ordered them. 'I want your best behaviour. Your very best. Remember that you are representing the school. If you remember that, then you will not fail to behave in a civilised manner. A civilised manner. That is the ethos of our school.'

When they had all marched dutifully in, the huge door shuddered and slowly closed again. Bryant helped keep the children in order at the back of the crowd.

'You can't do this!' cried Miss Lauren. 'You can't!' These were her children and she loved them dearly. It was shocking enough to see how enormous they had become but the thought that they were going to their deaths was too much for her. She struggled again at the ropes but they were tied too tightly.

'You monster!' shouted Mrs Jones, her anger bursting out. If she could get free she would gladly give her own life to destroy this witch and save those helpless children.

'Why are you doing this?' demanded David. 'Are you doing it just because you're a witch? There's no need! I'll serve you with devotion but please spare them!'

The witch was impressed with this plea. She liked to hear her victims plead with her; it added something to the pleasure of the work.

'On with the grinders! On! On!' she commanded and the huge teeth went spinning round with a deafening roar. And as they spun faster and faster, the anger of the demon's face turned furious, sucking the points of light into its dark mouth. The entire apparatus tilted forward and aimed itself towards the waiting children. Anything or anyone who so much as touched them would be sucked in and ground to a pulp in the blink of an eye. The remains would be hurled at speed into the gigantic industrial cauldron to be mixed with the special sickly powder into a meaty, greasy paste.

'Isn't it fantastic, children?' cried Mr Williams in an ecstasy of admiration. 'I very much hope you're grateful for the privilege of being here. Line up properly now. Everyone will get their turn but I must have order.'

As Mr Williams fussily herded the children into an orderly queue, the witch pulled a lever, releasing a huge quantity of the powder from the canister down the tube and into the cauldron. The odour of it reached David's nostrils, revolting him further. The children became excited and difficult to manage as the smell reached them. Mr Williams huffed and puffed and shouted for order but the smell was having its effect on him as well. Perhaps, he thought to himself, he should be the first to inspect the grinders. That would be his duty as headteacher.

'Remember who's in charge of the grinders,' shouted the witch above the noise. 'He's the one who turned the switch.'

'Only because you made him do it!' shouted David back to her.

'He's just doing it like a robot!'

'But he's the one who's doing it just the same,' gloated the witch.

'Why?' cried David. 'Why are you doing this?' Then he remembered the burnished silver mirror he had seen in her house. That showed the best side of people – and it was in her bedroom.

'What about the mirror?' he demanded. The witch looked at him intently.

'You've got that mirror in your bedroom. It shows good things. You must spend a lot of time gazing into it.'

'Oh, I do. I do.'

'Then there must be some good in you. Something to make you want goodness. What is it you see? What is it? We can help if you just ask.'

The witch considered for a moment. His words had made a deep impression on her. He was cleverer than she thought. She stroked her chin and her face softened as she bent down to cup his face in her bony hand.

'Oh, child,' she said softly. 'I do see the good in the mirror and I do yearn for it. What I see in that mirror is good. So very, very good.' She paused and then her voice suddenly changed and she stood up straight and clenched her fist right in front of his face.

'I see my power,' she shouted. 'My absolute and complete power in all its glory and it is beautiful and good.'

David struggled with his bonds and pleaded with her. 'You have power. You can have anything you want without all this killing!'

'But the slaughter is my power. It makes me what I am!' retorted the witch. 'All those children down there are my little pigs. I've fattened them up and now I'll turn them into meaty paste. First you fatten your pigs and then you process them.'

All three of them turned away in disgust as the witch continued: 'I will make these children into a delicious fatty food, for sale at a very cheap price. Cheaper than any other food. Perhaps I might offer free toys as well. Something to get the children interested and involved. All the world will love my food and will crave it above all else. Soon nobody will want to eat anything but my food.'

'But that means killing more and more children!' protested David.

'Yes,' the witch agreed. 'This is just the beginning.

Soon there will be factories like this in every part of the world. And then larger and larger factories full of slaves and I will have everything I could ever want – the absolute power to do my evil!'

'You'll get found out!' shouted David. 'They'll find out what's in the food and then you'll get what you deserve!'

'Yes, I will get what I deserve,' countered the witch. 'And I'll make sure that they do find out. When I am sure that everyone has eaten some of my food, I will tell them what it's made of. And they'll still want more of it. That will make them guilty and with guilt like that, they will be powerless. The guilt and the desire for more will make them weak. All over the world parents will bring their children to me to be fattened up and made into more food. Now that's what I really call a family meal.'

'That won't happen!' shouted Mrs Jones.

'Shut up!' the witch shouted back. 'Soon, very soon, the world will be in my power! All shall live by my command in the empire of Mrs GwraK!'

'No!'

'No? No, Mrs Jones? And why not? Shall I tell you the future? The future is this: fat feeding on fat feeding on fat forever more! That is the future and the future belongs to me!'

'You've hypnotised too many people and it's all been too easy for you!' shouted Mrs Jones. 'It's made you think people are bad just because you can make them bad. You'll get what you deserve in the end because you're wrong.'

The witch glared at her. This Mrs Jones was such a thorn in her side. She knew things and said things the witch had no answer for.

'We'll see!' the witch spat at her. 'We'll see!'

Mr Williams was still having difficulty organising the children. 'I demand your best behaviour,' he shouted. 'For the pride of our school. Your best behaviour.'

With help from Bryant they were at last forming orderly ranks and the children were now ready to see the inner workings of the factory – by walking into the teeth of the spinning grinders. The witch shouted angrily at Mr Williams: 'Haven't you got those pigs ready yet?'

Mr Williams looked up at her in wonder. 'Pigs?' he asked. 'What pigs?'

She clenched her jaw and ground her stumpy teeth in frustration. That woman had managed to fluster her again.

'The children, Mr Williams! The children!' she exclaimed. 'Get them in there now! We haven't got all night!'

Mr Williams rushed to obey. Mrs GwraK had been very kind in arranging this little trip for the children. She'd worked so hard and done so much for them and he was keen to keep her happy. She'd been so gracious and full of charity.

'Now then children,' he told them. 'No pushing and shoving, and no rushing. We'll all have our turn. All of you now, move forward.' The children began walking neatly towards the spinning metal teeth.

'If we could get out of these ropes, we might be able to help them,' whispered Miss Lauren. 'It might be possible to stir them up in some way. If we could just get out of these ropes!'

But all the while this was going on, something strange had happened to David's dad. The witch had fed him those biscuits and he'd been hypnotised to obey her. From then on he couldn't help it. Whatever she told him to do, he did it, as if in a dream. He stood by the switch, ready to turn on the grinders. But now, this other voice kept ringing in his ears:

'Dad! Dad, please! It's me, David! Please don't! Dad! Dad! She's a witch! Dad! Dad!'

Every now and then this voice would become too much for him and he would stop what he was doing and try to work out who it was. Somewhere inside him he felt he should listen to it but he had to obey the witch.

'On with the grinders! On! On!' she'd shouted down to him. He knew his job. He flicked the switch that set the massive grinders spinning and the high-pitched screeching noise struck him full force. For a moment he was thrown out of his hypnotic trance and his son's voice pierced the confusion of his mind.

'Dad! Dad, please! It's me, David! Please don't! Dad! Dad! She's a witch! Dad! Dad!'

With a sudden shock he realised where he was and what he was doing. David! David was in danger! He clenched his fist to smack the grinders off but stopped himself just in time. If he turned the grinders off, the witch would know something was wrong and she'd come to investigate. He wasn't foolish enough to believe he could confront and defeat a witch. She would hypnotise him again and that wouldn't help anyone. He looked down at the children. They would die if he didn't switch them off. But they would die anyway when the witch regained control of him. What could he do? The only hope was to use the noise of the grinders as cover, climb the network of metal struts to the next platform and release David, Mrs Jones and Miss Lauren. Together they might surprise the witch in time to warn the children.

He got a sharp knife from the toolbox and climbed the framework until he reached the three of them. By this time the witch was berating Mr Williams and telling him they didn't have all night.

David's father whispered: 'Shshsh, David. It's me. I'm alright now. I'll cut you all free and then we'll attack.'

David was filled with a renewed hope. His dad

was alright again and he was going to save them. He quickly cut the ropes then jumped over the railings onto the platform. The witch spun round but the first thing she saw was Mrs Jones rushing at her. With all the strength that years of lifting heavy pots had given her, the dinner lady grabbed the witch and pushed her against the railings of the platform. All the wind was knocked out of her and her arms were pinned down by Mrs Jones who shouted down:

'Mr Williams! It's me, Mrs Jones!'

Mr Williams looked up in amazement. Mrs Jones? What was she doing here? Was she attacking poor Mrs GwraK?

'I wouldn't go in there!' she shouted. 'I've poisoned it all! I've put frogs and snakes and cockroaches in there! Ha, ha, ha!'

She put on a wild, insane expression and leered madly at him. Panic erupted. All the children scrambled away from the grinder, pushing and shoving and screaming. Bryant tried to hold them back but they were too much for him. David could see what Mrs Jones was trying to do but he knew it wouldn't take long for the witch to recover and counterattack. They needed more chaos. His dad joined Mrs Jones in her struggle with the witch but she glared at him and David saw the grey flame flare up in her eyes. His dad stopped. Even though the witch needed her arms to direct her magic, she could hypnotise with her eyes alone and he'd already been under her spell.

'Get rid of this woman! Stab her with the knife!' she ordered him and obediently he lifted the knife to strike Mrs Jones. Miss Lauren leaped at him, knocking him off balance. David grabbed at his knife arm, pulling it down with all his weight. He shouted at him to wake up again. His dad struggled with the power of the witch but still he tried to strike Mrs Jones.

David caught a glimpse of the children below. Bryant was getting them in some kind of order. He'd calmed Mr Williams down and they were both persuading the children that Mrs Jones had been telling lies.

David shouted to them: 'Hey! I've got extra portions of food and I'm sharing with all of you! Come on up here. First come, first served!'

With a roar of delight that only the Golden Food could inspire in them, the children shoved their way towards the stairs leading up to the platforms. They pushed Bryant against the wall and he fell down. They trampled him as they stampeded to the stairs where they crammed and blocked each other before gradually squeezing their way upwards.

'Calm and dignity, children!' ordered Mr Williams. 'I want decency and courtesy and no shoving!' But he was pushed to the ground by Adrian's enormous bulk.

'Adrian! Stop! You're trampling me!' protested Mr Williams before the wind was squashed out of him. Adrian vaguely remembered something about honesty and how his headteacher liked the truth.

'Yes, sir,' he replied. 'I am trampling you.'

The cheek! The infernal cheek! It was an outrage. Mr Williams had no breath to squeak let alone shout at him. Then came the lads. They were after the Golden Food but they weren't going to miss a chance like this.

'Oooooff' groaned the headteacher as they stampeded over him. He couldn't even say 'Aaaaww!' Next came the goody-goody girls. How shocking. A man they'd learnt to respect was in a mess. One by one they stepped on him, digging their heels into him to emphasise their contempt.

'Girls! Girls!' He tried to remonstrate with them but they had their noses in the air and ignored him. After that the rest of the school simply clamoured over him, regarding him as just a nuisance, getting in the way of their Golden Food. When Gareth lumbered over him, lost his balance and fell on him, Mr Williams was finally out for the count.

David bit his dad's hand and he dropped the knife. David dived for it. But then he saw that Annette was still walking towards the teeth of the grinder.

'Annette!' he warned at the top of his voice but sensible Annette ignored him. Mr Williams had told her she was there to see the factory, especially the grinder, and that's exactly what she was going to do. She always ignored chaos – and this time it was going to cost Annette her life.

'Throw that woman off!' commanded the witch. David's dad threw Miss Lauren aside. As she fell against the railings she saw Annette calmly walking towards the grinder. She shouted down at her in her best teacher's voice:

'Annette! Where is your homework!'

The girl looked up at Miss Lauren. No teacher had ever talked to her like that. Her lower lip quivered. What homework? She didn't know there was any homework!

'Turn around and follow the other children!' ordered Miss Lauren and Annette obeyed. The teacher was always right.

The witch struggled out of Mrs Jones' grasp. With her hands free, she directed her magic at Mrs Jones and she fell back. Now the witch held her and Miss Lauren in her power and David knew he had to do something drastic. He jumped towards the tube filled with sickly powder and stabbed at it with the knife. It was made of a soft, thin metal and it cut quite easily. He sawed at it and the gash grew and grew. Some powder puffed out of the breach but David ignored his revulsion.

'Stop him!' ordered the witch when she realised what he was up to. His dad grabbed David and pulled him back. He'd only cut halfway through the tube.

'I've had enough of this!' said the witch. 'Hear no voice but mine and strangle the boy!'

'No!' David pleaded with his dad but his voice couldn't reach him. He turned his son around and despite the kicking and struggling, placed his hands around his neck.

'Dad! No, dad! No!' screamed David but his words were cut off by the choking pressure on his throat.

'Your only hope of escape,' gloated the witch, 'is to stab your father with the knife. Kill him or he will kill you!'

David felt the knife in his hand.

'That's right my child,' goaded the witch. 'You must do it! You must!'

He lifted the knife up and up. He showed it clearly to his dad. There was a flicker of realisation that the knife meant danger but still he clenched his fingers tighter around his son's throat. With one last pleading look to his father, David threw the knife clanging to the floor. That was enough. The surprising action and the sudden noise lifted his dad just enough out of his trance to see what he was doing. He let go and David fell to the floor. The struggle inside his father was clear. Any moment now the witch would put him back under her control and David would have no escape.

Just then, the doctor came bounding up one of the stairways. He had been on the platform below unaware that anything was wrong and happily waiting for the slaughter to begin so that he could switch on the mixers. The grinders were turning and there was a lot of shouting – just as he'd expected. Then suddenly the platform had begun to vibrate strangely and a hoard of children came rushing towards him. In a panic he'd rushed up to tell the witch.

'They've escaped!' he puffed. 'What do we do?'

The platform started to vibrate with a great rumbling sound.

'What do we do?' repeated the doctor.

'Silence!' commanded the witch. 'I'm going to set things right once and for all.' She stretched out her arms and splayed her fingers to encompass all the stairs.

'Stop children!' she shouted and the rumbling and vibrating ceased just as the first of the children reached the platform.

'Return below!' she ordered and the children turned quietly around.

This was the end for David. They were all so tired and the witch was restoring order and calm where David had tried to cause chaos. His dad was free from the witch for now; she was too distracted with other problems. He turned to look at her and saw her as she really was for the first time. She made a great target with her arms outstretched. She was asking for it and it was irresistible. With all his might David's dad smashed against the tube. It was already sliced in half and when he whammed against it the thin metal sheared in two. A massive jet of sugar shot out at great speed, blasting the witch back against the railings. As the giant cloud spread out, it blocked everything from view like a thick fog.

The witch clung to the railings to stop herself being thrown into the teeth of the grinder. The doctor and the children went wild as they were immersed in a pure mist of their very favourite flavour. They tried to eat the air and catch the powder on their tongues. They tried to grab great handfuls of it and licked their fingers with great globs of drool. The witch, trapped in the blast of powder, couldn't control them. Mrs Jones and Miss Lauren coughed and spluttered and tried not to swallow any of the stuff. David found his dad who was just struggling to his feet.

'Don't be taken in by the sweetness. It's dangerous,' warned David. But his dad had never tasted such a flavour before. It was even better than those biscuits.

'If you don't resist the sugar then we'll all be dead.' His dad kept licking his lips.

'You'll be the one who kills us… who'll kill me!' He stopped licking his lips. The muscles of his jaw clenched as he willed himself to resist the lure of the sugar. At last he nodded. He was ready.

'Come on,' he said to David, and together they climbed down to the lower platform.

The sugar wasn't as dense here but the air was

still misty with it. David's dad took him to the switch that controlled the mixer. There was a thick, black cable leading to it. He grabbed a screwdriver from the toolbox and started unscrewing the wire from its brackets.

'This cable carries 25,000 volts of electricity,' he explained. 'If this doesn't do the job, nothing will.'

Above them and on the stairs the commotion was becoming a frenzy. The children were crowded onto the top platform, fighting to get at the jet of sugar.

David's dad worked quickly to remove the brackets and once he'd succeeded, he took the cable and ripped the rest of it off the wall. There was a good length of it now, enough to reach the witch. Then he got to work releasing the cable from the switch.

Out of the corner of his eye, and through the sugary mist, David saw the shadowy form of Bryant approaching.

'Dad!' he warned. 'It's Bryant. A servant of the witch!'

David thought that if Bryant attacked his dad, the policeman would win. He was trained and his dad had never been in a fight as far as David knew. Then he felt his dad grab him by his collar and shake him violently.

'Slay the enemies of Mrs GwraK,' said his dad in a dead voice.

'Dad!' David protested but it was no use. Through the mist he could see his dad's glazed expression.

'No, dad! No please!' pleaded David. They'd got so close to success, and now this.

'What's going on?' asked Bryant sharply, coming near enough to see them clearly. He was in a terrible state having been trampled by the children.

'Slay the enemies of Mrs GwraK,' said David's dad again.

'Carry on,' smirked Bryant. His smirk grew into a grin and that's when the industrial-sized spanner struck him on the side of the head. He sank to the platform floor like a heavy sack.

David looked up at his dad who chucked the spanner aside. He winked at David.

'Your dad knows a trick or two as well,' he laughed. Then he unscrewed the cover of the switch and released the cable. He held it very carefully. It hummed with electricity.

'I've taken the cable from the mixer instead of the grinders,' he explained. 'That way, the witch won't notice anything different and she won't expect this attack.'

David nodded that he understood but just then, the rumbling stopped and the fog of sugar cleared. The crush of children and the jet of powder had kept the witch at bay for a while. But now she had worked herself free and commanded the jet of sugar to stop. There was a disappointed groan from the children as they stood licking the empty air.

'Back down the stairs!' she commanded.

All the children shuffled off sadly. The grinders still hummed but the witch saw that the doctor was trampled unconscious. That was a nuisance. She would have to gather her servants together, get Mr Williams to obey her commands properly, recapture her enemies and fulfil her plan to turn her fattened pigs into a delicious fatty food.

She glared threateningly at Miss Lauren and Mrs Jones. They were hanging from the railings of the platform. They could stay there for now. They were too tired and frightened to be a threat to her.

'Bryant!' she called. 'Bryant! Where are you?' But she got no answer from him. He was out cold.

David and his dad had kept in the shadows as the children went past. But on hearing the voice of the witch, his dad gripped him by the shoulder.

'I'm sorry, David. I can't do this.'

David turned to look at him.

'What?'

'She'll be calling for me next and I won't be able to resist.'

'But dad! You have to do it! You're the only one who knows how!'

They heard the witch calling out again for Bryant. David's father pleaded with his son. 'I can't, David. I'm sorry.' He handed the cable over but David didn't want to take it.

'But I can't do it alone,' he cried. 'Dad, I need you. I can't face her alone!'

'You have to.'

They heard the witch call out for David's father and a change came over him. A kind of spasm. His face was contorted with pain as he tried to resist the power of the witch.

'Take it, David. Take it now while there's still time!' His hands were shaking with the strain.

'Please, dad. Fight it! Fight it for me! I need you!'

But the witch called out again, her voice sterner this time. His face relaxed and the dull, glassy, hypnotised look returned to his eyes. David snatched the cable from him. He knew this time he might have to kill his father to get at the witch and he was filled with a sorrow so deep he could have just sunk to his knees there and then and given up.

But there was still just a glimmer of his old dad in the eyes. It was fading fast but he was still fighting to be himself.

'I'll do it, dad. I'll do it.'

'Good luck,' he said. 'And I'll distract her for you.'

With that, he ran beneath the upper platform and down one of the stairs towards ground level. The witch heard his footsteps and shouted: 'Stop!'

He stopped instantly.

'Well at least I've found you,' she said, unaware that David was slowly sneaking up the other steps with the cable.

'Find your son and bring him to me,' she ordered.

He resisted the command even though her words

flooded his mind and blocked all other thoughts. Slowly, David climbed the stairs, hoping the cable was long enough.

'Do you hear me?' screamed the witch, unable to put up with even a moment's defiance. 'Find your son and bring him to me!'

He turned and walked, hypnotised and dazed, towards where he knew David would be. His only thought now was to stop his son and bring him before the witch.

David reached the platform and saw the witch with her back to him. He had to be extra careful as he sneaked closer and closer to Mrs GwraK. Mrs Jones and Miss Lauren hid their surprise at seeing him. There was only a little slack left of the cable and David could tell it just wouldn't reach her. He pulled it as tight as he could but it wasn't enough. It was just a foot too short. The witch was about to turn round before David was ready so Mrs Jones racked her brain for some way to distract her.

His dad found the cable and followed its trail up the stairs. He moved slowly under the influence of the hypnosis but step-by-step, he was getting closer.

'Umm,' said Mrs Jones, thinking and thinking what to say to get the witch's attention. 'There are all sorts of bad foods,' she said at last.

'What?' exclaimed the witch. What was this stupid old woman babbling on about now?

'For instance,' continued Mrs Jones. 'There's fried food.'

David's dad reached the platform, his son only a few feet away from him.

'Fried what?' said the witch above the noise of the grinders.

'No, no,' said Mrs Jones. 'Not fried what. Fried witch.'

'What?' said the witch.

'Fry the witch! Fry her David! Fry her!'

The witch spun round and saw David. Her arm shot out to point her magic at him and David froze. With her arm pointing at him she was within reach, but he couldn't move. Then she saw his dad approaching and she gave a smug smile of victory. David was about to be caught and captured by his own father.

'You heard Mrs Jones!' shouted Miss Lauren, using her best teacher's voice again. 'Fry her, David! Fry the witch!'

That did it. Years of daydreaming in class had taught him to obey that voice. With his dad just about to grab him, he touched the witch on her finger with the end of the cable and 25,000 volts of electricity coursed through her veins. Her blood boiled and her skin sizzled. Her eyes, staring straight at David, almost popped out of her head.

'No-o-o-o-o!' she screamed. 'You are my servant! Obey me!'

She shot up in the air like a rocket, trailing smoke. She smashed against the factory roof and fell. She bounced off several of her staircases, dragging

cobwebs with her. She landed, screaming, in the teeth of the grinder. Her scream turned to a whimper as the teeth caught her. The machine groaned with the strain as all her power was focused on stopping the teeth. She looked up at David with a pleading look in her eyes. He looked back down at her and for the first time saw her as a real, living person.

'How can you feel so... so sorry for yourself?' he shouted at her. It was the only way to defeat the pity that welled inside him at the sight of those pleading eyes. With his words, her expression changed to a look of such savage hate that David felt the force of it quivering in his bones. But her final trick, to make him sorry, had failed. She was sucked into the teeth, into the dark mouth of her demon machine and spat out in a pulp, into her own giant cauldron filled with her own vile savoury sugar.

recovery

The lunch bell rang and all the children except David and Annette groaned. Nobody much liked David at lunchtime. They only had a vague memory of what had happened to them, but they all knew they'd been eating this delicious Golden Food and David had spoilt it for them. Because of him, they had to eat ordinary food now and it wasn't fair.

But it wasn't all bad for David. Gareth and the rest of his friends had started talking to him and had decided to forgive him for not sharing his food. It wouldn't be long before they were all the best of friends again. Annette was the first to notice that they'd all somehow grown an extra layer of fat. She was only going to eat really proper food from now on. But she was far too sensible, really too extremely sensible, for anyone to follow her example.

Little by little all the children were getting rid of that layer and returning to their normal, different sizes. Adrian was never going to be thin and Gareth was never going to be tall and the variety in size, shape and character was returning to the school. The children shuffled past David, and the goody-goody girls who were always so very, very good gave him their very best snub. David had somehow been naughty and nobody liked him, so they looked down on him with contempt.

Miss Lauren gave him a knowing look, as if to say, 'Don't worry, some of us know the truth'. David smiled back. His favourite teacher was back in school and Mrs Jones was making the meals again.

Bryant and the doctor had been taken away and locked up. They had been true servants of the witch, not just hypnotised drones, mindless and obedient. His dad had returned to his old job but now they offered him all kinds of promotion and better pay. They thought he was a hero and he let them shower him with money. He lectured them on the need for balance between life and work and they gave him extra holidays.

And what a shock his mum had when she learned the truth.

'Mrs GwraK?' she exclaimed over and over. 'That nice old lady? She was a witch? But she baked such lovely biscuits!'

For ages she just could not believe it. But when she did, at last, accept the truth she was very proud of her son, and so glad the danger was over. She hugged him so hard, and kept on hugging him with the force of an animal. He couldn't breathe with the tightness of the hug, until finally she released him. And her tears flowed.

As David made his way to the canteen he bumped into Mr Williams who was always a little embarrassed at seeing David these days. It was true David had saved the day but all his ten years' experience as a headteacher had taught Mr Williams a thing or two about boys – and this one in particular.

'Now look,' he said with a slight cough. 'It's true you've saved the school and the lives of everyone here and heroically killed a witch who was bent on evil world domination. But that's not an excuse for daydreaming in class, or not doing your homework, or getting into fights, or running out of the gates during school hours. I hope that's clear to you. Boys your age need to learn a lesson or you won't learn anything. Is that clear?'

He strode off to have his lunch. But there was nothing to worry about. David was never ever going to daydream again and he wasn't going to stare out of the window either. He'd done too much of that and it only ever got him into trouble.

beware

the Revenge of

Mrs Gwrak

Mrs GwraK is just one of a whole range of publications from Y Lolfa. For a full list of books currently in print, send now for your free copy of our new full-colour catalogue. Or simply surf into our website

www.ylolfa.com

for secure on-line ordering.

TALYBONT CEREDIGION CYMRU SY24 5HE
e-mail ylolfa@ylolfa.com
website www.ylolfa.com
phone (01970) 832 304
fax 832 782